IRELAND

From the Act of Union • 1800
to the Death of Parnell • 1891

*Seventy-seven novels and collections
of shorter stories by twenty-two*
Irish and Anglo-Irish novelists

selected by

PROFESSOR ROBERT LEE WOLFF
Harvard University

A GARLAND SERIES

Traits
and Confidences

Emily Lawless

with an introduction by
Robert Lee Wolff

Garland Publishing, Inc., New York & London
1979

For a complete list of the titles in this series,
see the final pages of this volume.

This facsimile has been made from a copy in
the Princeton University Library (3822.1.391).

The volumes in this series are printed on acid-free,
250-year-life paper.

Library of Congress Cataloging in Publication Data

Lawless, Emily, Hon., 1845–1913.
Traits and confidences.

(Ireland, from the Act of Union, 1800,
to the death of Parnell, 1891)
Reprint of the 1897 ed. published by Methuen, London.
I. Title.   II. Series.
PR4878.L6T7   1979   823'.8   78-24498
ISBN 0-8240-3524-0

Printed in the United States of America

The Irish Fiction of
the Honourable Emily Lawless

Emily Lawless (1845–1913)[1] was the second child and
eldest daughter of the third Lord Cloncurry and so a
granddaughter of the second peer, who, as Valentine
Lawless, had been a sympathizer with the United
Irishmen of 1798 and an opponent of the Union with
England in 1800–1801. He was twice imprisoned. It
was his father who left the Catholic Church,
conformed to the Church of England, was elected to
Parliament, and was created first a Baronet (1776)
and then a Baron (1789). The family, then, were
relatively recent recruits to the Ascendancy. Emily
Lawless' mother was the beautiful Elizabeth Kirwan
of Castle Hackett, County Galway, who found herself
with full responsibility for their nine children when
her husband died in 1859. Emily was then fourteen.
Part of the year the family lived at Maretimo House,
the family residence near Dublin, and the rest of the
year in her mother's native Galway.

As a child, Emily Lawless was an avid reader and
enjoyed memorizing long passages of Elizabethan
plays. Once when her father asked her to give her
latest recitation to an evening party of his fellow
sporting squires, she obliged by declaiming a long
blank verse diatribe delivered by a husband to his

faithless wife, in which each line ended with the word *whore,* a word she liked but of whose meaning she had not the faintest idea. The gentlemen did, however, and enjoyed the performance until her father gently turned her off ("Thank you, Emily; very nice, but that is enough"). But her real passion was for nature. She became an excellent amateur entomologist and botanist. In *Traits and Confidences* (1897; No. 75 in this series) will be found an entertaining reminiscence of her pursuit (aged ten) of a rare moth. Miss Lawless' accurate observation of the Irish landscape and of the sea in all seasons and all weathers became a notable feature—unobtrusive but immensely effective—of her fiction, when she began to write in the early 1880's under friendly prompting from the success-ful and enormously prolific Scottish novelist Mrs. Oliphant. Her first fiction was set in England, but it was her Irish stories that made her famous in her lifetime and deserve revival now.

Hurrish. A Study (2 vols., Edinburgh, 1886; No. 71) was her third novel and the first about Ireland. Set in the region known as the Burren, a beautiful portion of the Atlantic coast in northern County Clare, where the landscape appears desolate, but rich grass growing amidst the rocks provides good fodder for sheep and cattle, *Hurrish* tells the story of a peasant. Hurrish is a good man and a peaceful one, whose mother, a fierce old harridan, feels "shame" because her son is so averse to violence, but who nonetheless kills and is killed in circumstances wholly Irish and entirely convincing. His family—including his chil-dren, his gentle virtuous sister-in-law, even his dog—all ring true, as do the parish priest and the village idiot. Of course, Miss Lawless was looking at the peasantry from outside; about that she had no choice. But her understanding and sympathy seem to have been boundless.

In the 1880's, with Land League agitation rising and replacing the activities of the secret societies so often encountered in the earlier fiction in this series, we find Hurrish scorning and detesting the "Land-grabbers," the new men who have profited by the Encumbered Estates Act to acquire land. But he still retains a "sneaking regard" for the "ould stock, the aboriginal landlord, so to speak," men like Pierce O'Brien, who resides on his estates, who does not press for his rents, who takes personal care of everything about his property, but who is nonetheless widely detested just because he *is* a landowner. Miss Lawless' depiction of O'Brien and of the sad fate he incurs because of the greed of other men serves as a late commentary on the practicality of Edgeworthian principles: Maria Edgeworth would have wholly approved of O'Brien and found herself unable to understand the circumstances that had rendered her precepts invalid. The farrier, Phil Rooney ("a finished gentleman if self-respect and the most perfect breeding in the world are the essentials"), can remember the Famine and, of course, the failure of Fenianism. Like Hurrish, he too has no use for "the modern generation of agitators."

But Hurrish and Rooney are almost alone now, "like the elk or the old Irish wolf-hound," says Miss Lawless, reverting to the symbols of Irish antiquity used by the novelists since Maria Edgeworth. The newer generation, half-educated, with Americanized aspirations, form a wholly different breed. In the end, Hurrish must die because "Hate of the Law is the birthright and the dearest possession of every native son of Ireland ... because for many a year that country had been as ill-governed a morsel of earth as was to be found under the wide-seeing eye of God." *Hurrish* appeared in 1886, the year of Gladstone's effort to put through Irish Home Rule, and of its failure amidst rising agrarian discontent. Everybody was thinking about Ireland. *Hurrish* gave the public a new and sympathetic and knowledgeable view of some of the major Irish problems, while emphasizing past English misgovernment and neglect. *Hurrish* was widely hailed and Miss Lawless' next novel eagerly awaited.

After a competent one-volume history of Ireland (1887), she published *With Essex in Ireland* (1890; No. 72), ostensibly a firsthand account written as a journal by a participant in the Earl of Essex' expedition to Ireland in 1599 as Queen Elizabeth I's Lord Lieutenant. Essex' mission was to subdue Hugh O'Donnell, the rebellious Earl of Tyrone. The diarist, Essex' secretary, Henry Harvey, writing in pleasant Elizabethan prose, records Essex' march from Dublin southwest to Cahir and the return to Dublin by a roughly parallel route lying south and east of the outward journey, followed by a sortie northwards into Louth and a meeting with O'Donnell. So convincingly did Miss Lawless do her work as an imitator of Elizabethan style that many of her readers were convinced that she had discovered and edited an important new document, instead of writing a historical novel. Even Mr. Gladstone, learned man, student of Ireland, and inveterate novel reader though he was, was taken in. When he found out the truth, he was all the more excited and piqued. He could not wait to meet Emily Lawless and knocked on her hotel room door while she was staying at Cannes. She was lying on her bed with her shoes off and in her dressing gown, and thought the knock was that of a waiter bringing her tea. Horribly embarrassed at being discovered slightly dishevelled by the three-times Prime Minister, she was delighted when he sat down in her room and talked to her uninterruptedly for two hours about Ireland.[2]

With Essex in Ireland, sticking closely to the facts of sixteenth-century history, is also a pointed commentary on the entire disastrous history of Anglo-Irish relations. Among the fierce Elizabethan Englishmen, sure of their superiority to the wild Irish, Essex and the diarist, Henry Harvey, emerge as decent and relatively humane. Gradually their experiences teach them that the Irish are more than savages, bearers of a Celtic culture that the Englishmen cannot understand but that leaves them in awe. It is easy to understand, therefore, how greatly the book appealed to Yeats, who in 1895 included it in his list of the thirteen best books of Irish fiction.[3] Miss Lawless herself later said of it, "The true hero, or rather heroine, is the wretched country itself, groaning under its troubles, and yet with that curious fascination which we all feel," and added that it was her favorite among her own books, since she was able to imagine that it was *not* by her.[4] A modern reader is likely to share Yeats's view of it.

Grania. The Story of an Island (2 vols., 1892; No. 73)

is set on Inishmaan, the middle island of the three Aran islands in Galway Bay, opposite the Burren, scene of *Hurrish*. Here life is even simpler and starker. The time of the action—the 1860's—has no particular importance; unlike *Hurrish, Grania* is not a novel in which political considerations play a role. The infertile, storm-swept, and often fogbound rock, to which a few inhabitants cling, is a universe in itself, within which Miss Lawless introduces only three chief characters: Grania, her sister, and her suitor. The changing of the seasons and the vicissitudes of the weather provide the events that govern their lives. The two incidents in which the outside world impinges—a visit to the Galway fair and the momentary landing of three tourists on the island—serve only to emphasize Grania's isolation. Her fate is pure tragedy made the more poignant by her own realization that it is inevitable. Reflection on what might have happened had Miss Lawless given her plot a different turn suggests that the tragedy—which Grania herself fully understands—would only have been more protracted and more agonizing.

None of the personages ordinarily speaks in English, so Miss Lawless does not give them a brogue. Instead she "translates" their Irish speech into a musical form of English that effectively suggests the difference between the two languages. Published six years before J. M. Synge's first visit to the Aran Islands and ten before his fourth, *Grania* as a novel challenges comparison with his celebrated journal, *The Aran Islands,* based on these sojourns. When *Grania* appeared, Miss Lawless received letters of praise from Viscount Morley, who compared her to

George Sand; from W. E. H. Lecky, historian of eighteenth-century Ireland, who became a close friend; from George Meredith; and from her admirer, Gladstone, now Prime Minister for the fourth and last time. Swinburne wrote her that he found it "one of the most exquisite and perfect works of genius in the language—unique in pathos, humour, and convincing persuasion of truthfulness."[5]

Two years after *Grania* came *Maelcho* (2 vols., 1894; No. 74), a second grim historical novel of sixteenth-century Ireland, set in the years 1579–1582, about two decades before Essex' expedition. The scene is Connaught and Munster, the protagonist an English youth who escapes a massacre of his noble Irish relatives by their Irish enemies and flees to Iar Connaught, the domain of the wild O'Flahertys. The description of tribal life in this desolate region south of Connemara is extremely well done. From this dangerous refuge, the hero escapes a second time southward into the hands of the Spaniards and Irish noble rebels against Elizabeth who are invading Kerry, and finally makes his way into the forces of the Elizabethan armies sent to restore order to the southwest. This they try to accomplish by wholesale murder and devastation, described in all its grisly horror.

Maelcho himself is the *seanachie* (historian, harper, bard, magician, influential counsellor) of Sir James Fitzmaurice, one of the "Geraldine" Irish rebels, relatives of the Earl of Desmond. The reader meets Maelcho only when he is already an old man, and the novel suffers from our having to take on faith the assurances of the influence and power he had wielded in his earlier life. Once he has been introduced, moreover, Miss Lawless divides her attention between him and her young English protagonist, so that the structure of the novel is flawed. Her portrait of the sinister Cormac Cas, *seanachie* of the O'Flahertys, tells us more about the role of the minstrel-adviser in Celtic tribal Ireland. There is also a vivid account of the mendicant friars, lineal predecessors of Carleton's Darby Moore in "The Midnight Mass" (*Traits and Stories, Second Series,* 3 vols., 1833; No. 35) and of the other mendicants that throng his pages. When Yeats expanded his February 1895 list of thirteen best Irish works of fiction to sixteen later in the year, he included *Maelcho*, which he had just read, giving Miss Lawless the same number of titles as the Banims. Only Carleton had more.[6]

Emily Lawless' last completed work of adult fiction about Ireland was the collection called *Traits and Confidences* (1897; No. 75) which included the autobiographical essay on her girlhood moth hunt, "An Entomological Adventure." Two tales of assassination, one set in 1798, the other contemporary with the book's appearance, a brief medieval romance, memories and a story of the Famine, and a tale of tragic mésalliance that ends—almost too late—in reconciliation make up a varied and a delightful small book, less finished than the longer fiction but no less arresting. *The Race of Castlebar* (1913) she did not complete. Shan Bullock finished it for her and supplied most of its Irish portion. We therefore do not republish it here. In addition to her fiction, she wrote a life of Maria Edgeworth (1904); *Gilly*, a children's book (1906); and several books of verse, including *The Wild Geese* (1902) and *The Point of View* (1909), a small volume published privately for the aid of the Galway fishermen. The University of Dublin gave her the honorary degree of D. Litt. in 1905.

Emily Lawless was a deeply patriotic Irishwoman, much influenced in her thinking by her cousin Sir Horace Plunkett (1854–1932), younger son of the sixteenth Lord Dunsany, who in his young manhood spent a decade ranching in Wyoming, and after some preliminary efforts founded the Irish Agricultural Organization Society in 1894, in support of agricultural reform, notably cooperatives. Its organ, the *Irish Homestead*, founded in 1895, to which George William Russell (AE) contributed and which he later edited, also published some of Emily Lawless' verse. A great admirer of AE, who after 1897 was one of the I.A.U's chief organizers and helped the cooperative movement grow in ten years to the number of 876 societies and an annual turnover of £3,000,000, Plunkett was a Unionist in politics. He was a Member of Parliament after 1895, and the moving spirit behind the Land Act of 1896 and the creation of the Department of Agriculture and Technical Instruction for Ireland. With his later successes and disappointments we need not deal here.[7] Emily Lawless took her lead from him. She did not believe Ireland was ready for Home Rule, but did criticize British policy sharply. This explains why some nationalists accused her of being "unfair" to the Irish peasant characters in her novels, and some conservatives accused her of being "unfair" to British Rule. In 1911 she wrote Plunkett that a leading member (whom she does not name) of the "Gaelic Theatre and circle" had written her that what she had written had "helped them." "I am not *anti-Gaelic* at all," she commented to Plunkett, "as long as it is only Gaelic *enthuse* and does not include politics."[8]

The last years of her life she spent in England, increasingly an invalid, still happy working in her garden, "a tall, almost angular" woman in an "almost shapeless gardening hat," intelligent, warm-hearted, open-minded, with a multitude of friends, intensely Irish.

Robert Lee Wolff

Notes

1. Emily Lawless does not appear in the *DNB:* clearly an oversight. The entry on her in *The New Cambridge Bibliography of English Literature,* III, 2nd edition (Cambridge: University Press, 1969), col. 1907, among "Anglo-Irish Poets," includes an unusually large number of errors; her first book, *The Chelsea Householder,* appeared in London in 1882 in three volumes; *Hurrish* (No. 71) originally was published in two volumes; *Major Lawrence, F.L.S.* (1888) was published in three volumes; and there are two separate entries, both garbled, for *With Essex in Ireland* (No. 72), the first edition of which is the 1890 Smith, Elder edition reproduced in this series. In the absence of any biographical study, the obituary in the *Times,* October 23, 1913, is useful; so is Edith Sichel, "Emily Lawless," *The Nineteenth Century,* LXXVI (July 1914), 80–100. It too has a good many inaccuracies, however.

2. Sichel, p. 86. Gladstone would become Prime Minister for the fourth time in 1892.

3. Stephen Marcus, *Yeats and the Beginning of the Irish Renaissance* (Ithaca and London: Cornell University Press, 1970), p. 285.

4. Sichel, p. 86.

5. Sichel, p. 85. This letter is not included in C.Y. Lang's six-volume edition of Swinburne's letters.

6. Marcus, p. 286.

7. See F. S. L. Lyons, *Ireland Since the Famine* (London; Weidenfeld and Nicolson, 1971), pp. 202–211 and *passim*.

8. Sichel, p. 87.

TRAITS
AND CONFIDENCES

TRAITS
AND CONFIDENCES

BY THE HON.

EMILY LAWLESS

METHUEN & CO.
36 ESSEX STREET W.C.
LONDON
1897

TO

𝔖. 𝔖.

Five of the following stories have appeared in various reviews and magazines, the editors of which have kindly allowed them to be republished.   The rest of the volume is new,

CONTENTS

The littel teller tells hys littel minde
In littel tales to readers colde or kinde,
Some in plaine wordes, and some in wordes more blinde,
So muche is tolde, yet muche remaynes behinde.

The Cunninge Craftsmanne.

A SONG OF HOBBIES

TELL me truly, gentles fair,
What begat our hobbies? Where
First they grew? What unseen care
Gave each little mind its share?
Tell me further, tell me true,
How they came to me and you?
From the earth, or from the air,
Or the mystic everywhere?
   Nay, nay. Who shall say?
Fortune's blindest gifts are they.

Were they bought, or were they found
In the air, or in the ground?
Were they lent us from on high,
Merry playthings of the sky?
Are they of immortal birth?
Or mere mortal things of earth?
For my weal, or for my woe,
Tell me, how do hobbies grow?
   Nay, nay. Who shall say?
Fortune's blindest gifts are they.

AN ENTOMOLOGICAL ADVENTURE

IRISH properties are reported to have their drawbacks, and it is very possible that they may have—for their owners.   For those who are not their owners, nor ever likely to become their owners, an Irish property—I can answer for it personally — is the most delectable of delectable play-grounds, or was so at a period a good deal nearer to the hale-and-hearty middle of the century than it is always pleasant in these days of its flagging dotage to remember.   Boy or girl, it mattered not which you were, provided that you kept within certain prescribed boundaries—boundaries probably marked in your own mind with the natural and charming pomposity of youth as " our grounds," " our land "—within those limits you were free to roam, as you would, on foot or upon pony-back, unchecked and unfollowed even from afar by protesting maid or scandalized

3

governess. Such, at least, was our own never-sufficiently-to-be-blessed experience.

Probably the highest heights of joy, the most transcendent depths of rapture, were only to be found upon properties whose inner circumvallation boasted of a bog ; a moderately uncut bog ; one rich in feathery tussocks and in bog holes of immeasurable depth, and unsurpassed capability in the way of fishing forth all sorts of slimy, crawling, black, and many-legged personages out of their oozy depths. Above all, a bog rich in an "esker," or heath-covered ridge, trending away, far as the eye could reach, into blue, unmeasurable distances, never yet trodden by the feet of the explorer, but remaining always a region full of bewitching suggestions, of haunting mystery, of dim, untravelled possibilities. A region from which no amount of after-familiarity ever entirely succeeded in stripping away the glamour.

This last quintessence of joy was not, as it happened, in those days attainable by the young person whose experiences I am about to relate. For all that, she was content. Until larger hopes and more spacious possibilities have arisen to awaken discontent, the soul satisfies itself reasonably enough upon the lesser ones, or so philosophers, both in or out of short

frocks, have at various ages of the world discovered.

By what good fortune for herself, by what
ill-fortune for those whose duty it was to
"tidy up" after her, the love of "creatures,"
of "natural history," as in more dignified years
we term it, came to fall like a gift from the
gods upon that particular short-frocked philosopher's path, I cannot now delay to inquire.
Legends survive of feloniously introduced lady-
birds, and treacherously concealed grasshoppers,
which hopped in the dead hours of midnight
upon nursery carpets, and even across the
persons of innocently sleeping bed-fellows, but
these, one must trust, are not true. One still
darker tale survives of a small, but, I am
assured, exceptionally clammy frog, which having been carried in a hot little hand till it could
be carried no longer, was placed in the widely
open neck-frill of a younger brother, which
presented itself as a suitable receptacle, from
whence it rapidly travelled first to the victim's
neck, and next downhill over his entire remonstrating person, until it finally regained
daylight and liberty somewhere in the neighbourhood of his shoes and socks.

Of these earlier misdoings all I can say is
that the culprit herself has no recollection of

them.   Nine years old remains fixed in her
mind as the period at which the propensity
burst—literally and most unfiguratively burst—
beyond farther hope of concealment, revealing
itself not alone in overflowing buckets, baskets,
tin pails, and similar receptacles, but, what was
regarded as a great deal more scandalous, in
bulging and discoloured pockets, out of which
came creeping, crawling, buzzing, croaking,
chirruping, and, no doubt, generally remonstrating gentry, not usually counted as part
of "a good little girl's" natural properties or
reasonable " pets."

By way of for a moment interrupting these
biographical details, I may be allowed here to
remark that nine years old has always seemed
to me to be the really culminating moment,
the true pinnacle of human ambition.   At that
favoured age babyhood, with its petty restric-
tions and humiliating sense of feebleness, is past
and done with.   The first horrors of irrational
panic—that chill, nipping dread of we know
not quite what, which lurks in the blood of
nearly every son and daughter of Eve—is also
passed, or you pretend that it is, which comes
to much the same thing in the end.   On the
other hand, the first premonitory chill of dis-
illusion, and what is of still more importance,

the first numbing sense of your own unaccountably imposed limitations, are both alike far off. Life spreads itself before you, large, and broad, and long, and sunny. Birds sing, insects buzz, the very stars overhead twinkle encouraging remarks, addressed to you, and to you alone. Such at least is the theory. It may be a true or it may be a false one, but my own impression is that the closer it is examined the more reasonable will be found to be the grounds for its adoption.

As a corroboration of that theory, as well as by way of returning, as we all love to do, from the general to the particular, I may mention that the subject of the following adventure still recalls a day, in the course of that happy year of hope and blossom, when, becoming temporarily possessed of a copybook, destined for more practical, if also lowlier ends, she inscribed, in a handwriting of quite incredible shakiness and illegibility, the names of three snail-shells, two butterflies and four moths—copied out of Lardner's *Cabinet Encyclopædia*, with spelling variations of her own —also of a limestone fossil, a piece of feldspar, a fragment of mica, a stone celt, benevolently bestowed by some one, and a piece of plumpudding stone—set down as " Conglomerate."

After which effort, pausing for a moment to survey her achievement, and swelling with natural pride, as a suitable crown to her labours she inscribed above the rest, in a handwriting even more tottering and elementary than what had gone before, *The Union of all the Sciences*, by ——, her own name in full, with a calm certainty of achievement, a deep indwelling sense of recognized benefit to humanity, which a Newton or a Darwin might have envied, but which neither of them could possibly have surpassed.

And yet are mortals ever destined to stand upon the topmost peaks of self-satisfaction? Even for this aspiring naturalist, for this embryo discoverer, life had its drawbacks. If less pressing upon her than upon others, there still were certain respects in which the long-recognized limitations of her sex continued to assert themselves. The most formidable, perhaps, of these was the early recognition of the fact that under no circumstances, by no possible stretch of indulgence, would this coming Cuvier or Buffon in short frocks ever be entrusted with a gun! This plainly tyrannical, and heartless regulation had the natural effect of curtailing at one fell swoop the entire realm over which her future activities were to range, and in which she was to record her triumphs. Although, despite this humiliating restriction, woods, flower-beds, kitchen-garden walks, the back of the stables, the croquet ground, the rabbit yard, and other probable places were still daily scanned in full expectation that some bird or quadruped "new to science" would shortly present itself for her to discover, still by degrees she began to see that the wider fields being interdicted, it would be necessary to confine herself within narrower ones. From this cause it came to pass that winged insects, especially butterflies, and, close behind butterflies, moths, grew to occupy the foremost place in her affections, and from that day, for many a year to come, their education—as caterpillars — their capture, the exploration and contemplation of their haunts, habits, manners, customs, history, and civilization generally, became fixed in her mind, not only as the highest, but I may even go so far as to say the *only* really important object of human study. As for such puerile frivolities as were known to grown-up people as "accomplishments," as "the arts," "painting," "music," "literature," and so on, especially for such a visibly futile variation of the last as was summed up in school-rooms as "stories," and in drawing-rooms as "novels" or "romances,"—these, that short-petticoated Buffon swept into the dustbin with her scorn, and would as soon have thought of voluntarily returning to baby-bibs, or of going out riding with a leading-rein, as of ever, in the whole course of her life, deigning to occupy herself with them !

Although, to those unacquainted with its inner capabilities, entomology may appear to be a harmless, and even a reasonably safe entertainment, I would not have them take up that opinion too hastily. It is true that, compared with some of my heroine's earlier objects of ambition, it might claim to be so regarded ; yet I can assure the reader that it would never have been so dearly beloved as it was had it not afforded the very amplest opportunities for getting into mischief, especially if you happened to be a young person endowed with rather remarkable gifts in that direction. To walk out at dusk, for instance, with a bull's-eye lantern in your hand, along the tottering edge of some ivy-mantled ruin, where the difference between masonry and leaves is hardly perceptible even in the daytime, is a proceeding that abounds in very exciting moments, quite apart from the question of whether the ento-mologist returns home with full or empty pill-boxes ! The same bull's-eye lantern, carried along the naked top of a sea cliff, from over whose edge winged objects keep whizzing ; while a hoarse roar from the Atlantic booms in thunderous accents out of the void, and the ground yawns and quivers in unexpected places underfoot, is a yet more entrancing performance, but that particular form of rapture had not at this time grown to be part of our heroine's daily experiences.

Even where no such delectable opportunities as these presented themselves, there were no lack of occasions which offered a fair chance of breaking a leg or an arm. Then there was always the satisfaction of doing something that nobody else did; something that, if not exactly prohibited, was at least a source of a good deal of perplexity and inconvenience to those about you; something which had never been included in any school-room curriculum, and which no properly constituted governess could possibly think the better of you for doing! Apart from all this ; apart even from the out-of-door joys which it entailed, think of the dignity, of the sense of personal importance which such a pursuit conferred. Why, the very sonorousness of the name was worth anything ; a name which you secretly rolled round and round in your mouth, and applied to yourself as you walked about the house. What dignity, what majesty lay in its syllables—En-to-mo-lo-gist! Could anything be more entrancing?

But it is time to bring these discursive observations to an end, and come to the incident which was the only excuse for ever beginning them. Our Ambitious Entomologist's tenth birthday had been celebrated in the previous summer, and it was now getting to the middle of the following spring. It had been an extraordinarily long winter—at least a dozen years long, judged by later and less impatient standards—and she, like her betters, had been pining for the spring. Lardner's *Cabinet Encyclopædia* had in vain been turned over for the hundredth time, until its brightest plates had begun to lose their glow. She was pining for something more real than Lardner; pining to go out with a real net, real pill-boxes, and a real bull's-eye lantern, in search of real moths, but so far, unfortunately, there were no real moths abroad for her to go in search of. Day after day a bitter east wind blew, nipping back the spring, nipping down every creature endowed with anything of the nature of an epidermis. Our heroine, I imagine, cared little in those days about the east wind, but the moths apparently were wiser, and remained snugly ensconced within their chrysalides, waiting for the zephyrs that were to awaken them.

At last, late one evening, the weather changed suddenly. A warm wind came blowing in from the Atlantic, and as our Entomologist was going to bed, it reached her cheeks through an open window. Moreover, she saw that the upper part of that window was covered with small gnats, a sure sign, she knew, that moths were on the wing. Had it been a little earlier in the day her hat would have been on her head, and she would have been out, net in hand, in a twinkling. But, alas! it was bedtime, and mild as that government was under which she lived, still to that mildness there were limits, and to go out-of-doors at bedtime, would have been to pass beyond them. And yet, the pity of it! To think of going tamely to one's bed! To think of merely sleeping when one might be mothing! Think too of what chances might thereby be missed! Why, the "Great Unknown," the "New to Science" itself might be waiting for one outside there in the dark! might be actually sitting and staring with opalescent eyes from some tree trunk, and only kept from being secured by this ridiculous regulation of an eight o'clock bed hour!

Apart from the Great Unknown, which was sure to be always lurking somewhere in the background, there was a moth which, knowing no English name for it, our Entomologist had christened "The Whistler," from the noise it made when it flew. She had caught it once, and had vowed to herself that she would catch it again. Its time for flying was one hour after sunset, and again one hour before sunrise. Sunset being already past, sunrise was resolved upon, and upon that resolution she went to bed, and shortly afterwards fell asleep.

She awoke with a violent start. Light was streaming in at all the chinks of the window, and she felt with a pang that she had already overslept herself. Once the sun had passed a certain point in the sky, there would be no chance of catching "The Whistler," and surely the sun must already be quite high? Her clothes lay not far from her, and practice had made the getting into them a tolerably rapid proceeding. This feat accomplished, she stealthily opened her bedroom door, crept down the creaking staircase, and through the silent house. It struck her as she passed a passage window that the light looked a trifle white and odd, but she was too much occupied with trying to creep along unheard, to pay much heed to

such a detail as that.   In five minutes she had
reached a small side door, which opened out of
one of the wings, not far from the servants'
quarters.   It was locked, but the key was there.
She turned it ; pulled back a bar ; in a minute
the door was open, and she had darted out, shut-
ting it behind her.   Not, however, as she had intended to do, noiselessly, and discreetly.   On the
contrary, that inconsiderate door, slipping out
of her grasp, shut behind her with a portentous
bang, which, echoing through the house, seemed
bound to bring some one down to see who could
be disturbing it at so unseasonable an hour of
the morning.

Before its echoes had died away, our Entomologist was already at a considerable distance.
Fear of recapture, a sudden desire not to have
her errand known, lent wings to her steps, and
sent her speeding down the gravel walk, and
across the grass of the nearest paddock as fast
as her feet would carry her.   She had not gone
far, however, before she once more stopped
short, this time to stare open-mouthed at the
sky.   There, plainly to be seen, over the low
green top of the hill, and dipping towards the
lower end of the lake, was—not the sun, nothing of the sort, but the *moon*—the cold,
indifferent moon, the governess of floods, the

well-known enemy of all moths, and therefore of all moth-hunters. Here was a disaster! Here was a contingency quite unprovided for by Lardner. To meet with a setting moon where one looked to find a rising sun! Was ever more startling inversion of nature recorded by any perplexed naturalist! What was to be done? that was the question. Above all, what o'clock was it? that was the first and most important point to be decided.

This last question was answered with great promptness, for at that moment from the other side of the lake, the clock in the old castle struck distinctly "One, Two, Three." *Three!* In vain our Entomologist waited; in vain she besought the echoes to spare her even one hour more. They died away, leaving her staring before her at that serenely swimming, that horribly deceptive moon, which was now getting momentarily lower and lower, and threatening to leave her without even its exasperating light. Three o'clock! that meant two hours at least before anything like real honest daylight was to be looked for. Two hours! Who, looking back into the dim vista of his youth, cannot recall occasions when two hours seemed to stretch away with all the formidableness of a long and a most uncomfortable lifetime?

It was humiliating, it was disappointing, but there was no help for it, and her decision was quickly given to return to bed, the more so because, once her thoughts were allowed to run in that direction, the idea possessed an attraction which drew her towards it insensibly.   Quietly, therefore, she stole back across the grass, up the gravel walk, and once more reached the door by which her escape had been made.   She tried to open it; at first gently, then more energetically; she shook it; she turned the handle round and round.   Confusion and dire mischief!   It was once more securely locked! Some one, awakened by that unlucky clap, must have descended the servants' stairs, found the door open, and very properly secured it before returning to bed.   Here indeed was a calamity! What was our Entomologist to do?   Should she wake up the house; should she own to her blunder, and humbly ask to be taken in, or should she brave the matter out and remain where she was till daylight opened the doors? She was not afraid that any special alarm would ensue upon her not being found in her bed.   It was so much a matter of course for her to go for an early ride before the rest of the upstairs world were astir that it would not awaken any surprise if she was

c

found to have already gone out.   There remained, therefore, only the question of those
long hours of solitude which stretched away
before her—cold, and dull, and breakfastless
—hours which must somehow or other be got
through.

Pride, however, is a wonderful sustainer, and
the pride of our Entomologist had in those
days hardly any limits.   She made up her mind
that she would stay out, and would merely look
about her for some place in which to shelter
herself.   After all, one could always make believe that it was the afternoon, and who could
be so silly as to mind being out alone for a few
hours of an afternoon?

With this gallant resolution she marched
away, past various friendly doors, all of which
were now impenetrably shut and barred.   There
was the dairy, which in those days looked out
upon this side of the house.   What a tantalizing
smell of creaminess came floating through its
lattice-work to her nose!   There was the wood-
shed, there was the outer laundry, and there
were various other familiar haunts, all of which
were successively scanned, but, alas! to not
one of which was any entrance to be obtained.
To a now startled conscience, it was not a little
alarming to find how completely everything—

the whole scene, hitherto so familiar, so invariably kindly—seemed to have assumed a new
aspect, the aspect of a hostile citadel. The
very walls overhead seemed to have a different
look to-day ; seemed to frown down at her in
a cold, granitic fashion, with an angry gleam
in their innumerable mica eyes. The shut
windows, the locked doors, the very gravel
under her feet—everything seemed changed !
Everything wore a look of surprised displeasure;
everything seemed to be pointing and frowning
at her. It was all very fine to say that one
could pretend that it was the afternoon, or any
other reasonable hour. The conscience knew
better, and dragged down the spirits of that
prowler about at ungodly hours, to the very
soles of her saturated shoes.

At last a door was discovered to be open. It
was only the door of a pheasantry, which had
latterly been made into a home for certain
rabbits and guinea-pigs. Consisting entirely of
iron and wire-netting, with a roof which only
covered the inner portion, leaving an outer
parterre for the inmates to walk abroad in, it
was not the most comfortable place in which to
spend the chilliest hours of the twenty-four !
Still it had a roof, and our Entomologist accordingly unlatched the outer gate, and ran in
rejoicingly.

In her new-born need for companionship it was a comfort to her to reflect that she could now at least make sure of that of the rabbits and guinea-pigs ; persons who if on ordinary occasions she was apt to despise, would at least now break in upon this very tedious *tête-à-tête* with herself.   In that expectation she was, however, destined to disappointment. With a clearer perception of the time of day than she had shown, the rabbits and guinea-pigs alike declined to be seduced out of their morning's nap, merely shook their lop-eared heads or fat backs, and cuddled themselves down, with contemptuous squeaks, into their corners.

To our conscience-stricken wanderer this was a serious blow ! If your own rabbits—your mere paid pensioners, so to speak—thought your conduct inexcusable, what *must* other and less dependent beings think of it ? Under ordinary circumstances their judgments might not have troubled her, but this was very far from being an ordinary occasion.   There are hours of despondency when it is probable that the condemnation of a fitchew, nay of a polecat, would add a perceptible grain to the general account ! It was with a sense alike of hostile judgment and wounding ingratitude that our Entomologist laid her head against the bars of the pheasantry and dissolved into tears, in the middle of which

tears she was unexpectedly overtaken with
drowsiness, and fell asleep, her head still
resting against the bars.

For the second time she awoke with a violent
start. Where was she? In her own bed, where
else? Yet, no. Nothing could be less like
sheets and a pink quilt than what was at that
moment pressing against her neck. Then, if
not in bed, where was she? It happened just
then that the light was in the most uncanny
and uncomfortable condition it could well have
been in. Strong enough to show dim shapes and
adumbrations silhouetted against the sky, dark
enough to leave an appallingly black residuum
about the bases of those shapes; a blackness
which was like nothing natural, which seemed
to yawn and gape like "Tartar's vasty hell"
before the eyes of a very scared and shivering
small personage, out-of-doors by herself at four
o'clock in the morning!

Fear shook her from head to foot. The bars
seemed to be fetters, the pheasantry was a dun-
geon, the shapes outside those of ogres, as
powerful as cruel. A crowd of dim terrors,
boding and terrible, rose and clutched at her
with skeleton fingers. Bloodless faces gleamed
for a moment and then vanished. "Creep
things," of incredible size and hairiness, seemed

to be walking over her and tickling her with their myriad feet. This last was not a terror merely, but a humiliation as well, for if there was one thing upon which our ten-year-old naturalist prided herself, it was her absolute immunity from alarm of anything that walked or crawled—no matter upon how many legs.

Happily the daytime was now really approaching fast. It came with a rush of white films across the tree-tops; with a glad awakening twitter from every bush and ivied wall around. Cock pheasants began to crow, rooks passed to and fro overhead, wood-pigeons cooed from the hill wood, " Ill things of night began to peak and pine," as the honest daylight once more took possession of the scene.

With this return of daylight our Entomologist's courage began also to revive, for to be out-of-doors by herself was far too familiar a condition of things to occasion her any alarm. With the subsiding of the supernatural troubles the physical ones, however, began to make themselves felt. She was horribly cold, and how to get warmer she did not know. The clock across the lake had that instant struck five. It would be quite two hours before those inhospitable doors would be open. Where were those two chilly hours to be spent?

Suddenly she bethought her of the cowhouse. Would it be locked? She thought not; in any case it was not far off, and was worth a trial. Leaping to her feet she ran down the winding walk towards it; past the Bleach-green; past turn after turn, faster and faster, till she stopped, breathless and palpitating, before the cowhouse door.

Now, this cowhouse, to be candid, was not a clean, nay, was, I may say, a very muck-belittered place, and has long since been swept away as a mere blot upon an otherwise orderly landscape. In those days, however, it existed, and was very dear to the heart of our Entomo-logist, as well as to those of her immediate congeners. Its entrance lay under an arch lead-ing to a staircase. What a staircase! How creaking were its steps, how dark its corners, what dusky festoonings of cobwebs hung over it, what masses of hay fell upon you as you mounted it!

The loft to which this staircase led was the home of innumerable families of scam-pering mice, and its floor was riddled with holes, some of which holes—those above the heads of the cows—had probably made part of the design of the architect, while others, scat-tered vaguely here and there, could hardly

have been intentional. To throw down armfuls of hay through these holes upon the
fragrant noses of the inhabitants underneath
was a perennial pleasure. Some of the cows
were supposed to prefer their food rolled into
balls, and flung at them in that form, others to
like it best when it came in a shower, which fell
impartially over heads, horns, backs, and ground
below.   So liberal were the feeders that it
was really not a little marvellous that the
cows were not oftener startled by the descent
of the hay-givers, as well as the hay they
provided.

To get into that loft, and to nestle down in
it ; to breathe that warm, cow-scented air ; to
be comforted by the neighbourhood of those
big, friendly-eyed beasts, in place of the peevish,
thin-souled unfriendliness of the rabbits and
guinea-pigs, was a consummation after which
the soul of our Entomologist pined. Alas ! for
the third time that morning she found herself
baffled by Fate.   There was no lock to the door,
but there was a bar, and although that bar was
on the outside, it was drawn through its staple
with a strength and an ingenuity which rendered it quite immovable to a set of very chilled,
and not particularly strong little fingers. Pull
as they would, shake it as they would, it de-

clined to move, and again tears were very near breaking forth over this fresh unkindness.

Happily, at this melancholy moment an unexpected and a very consoling incident occurred. While vainly tugging at the bar, our Entomologist suddenly perceived that something soft and fluffy was moving away under her fingers. Her first impulse was to start violently, her next to close her fingers down over it, lest it should escape. Opening them cautiously, she perceived that it was a moth, and moreover a moth the like of which she had never seen before—a moth of the most vivid and dazzling green, save for a single bar of delicate fawn, which crossed it from tip to tip. What could it be? Had any one ever seen it before? Did Lardner know it? Had Mr. Newman or Mr. Doubleday—these were names which had just begun to come within her ken—ever seen the like? She felt perfectly certain in her own mind that not one of them had ever done so. Then, if not, it was *new!*—it was the long-looked-for, it was the "Unknown to Science," destined, from the beginning of things, to be discovered by her, and by her alone!

Diving into her pocket, she extracted from it a chip pill-box, which had been destined to contain "The Whistler." It was too small for the new captive, but with a little ingenuity she managed to get it in.   Pill-boxed, and safe in her pocket, she was able to face the world with the confidence of one who feels that her destiny has begun to fulfil itself.   To get indoors and to consult Lardner ; to make sure of her facts —though, indeed, she felt already sure enough —was now her great object.   Alas ! those two inexorable hours still remained, and still had to be got through.

Casting round in search of some shelter, her attention was suddenly arrested by a neighbouring haystack, a large one, containing the whole winter provender of the cows.   If she got under that haystack, and pulled a few armfuls of hay over her as a blanket, that at least would be better, she thought, than standing where she was.   Upon going towards it with that intention, she observed that a small hole a few feet above the ground had been left in the stack so that air might circulate through it.   The sight of this hole inspired her with a still better idea. Why not get into the stack itself?   If she could creep into it by that hole she could hardly fail to be warm enough, and could lie at her ease, and at full length.   No sooner thought of than carried into execution.   The hole was just out of reach, but some large stones were lying near, and by mounting upon the biggest of these our Entomologist managed to hook her elbows into the hole, and to pull herself up to it. A little more wriggling and kicking and she was inside, her whole body, with the exception of her feet, being comfortably tucked away in the hay.

The hole narrowed rapidly, but this she did not mind, reflecting it would only keep her the warmer. Her feet, however, being still cold, she pulled away the hay before her with her hands, until she had made a regular burrow for herself, and could lie in it at full length, feet and all. It was a very warm burrow, and, half numb with cold as she had been, the contrast was at first delicious, and she inly congratulated herself upon the brilliancy of this her latest and most successful idea.

Little by little, however, the hole, at first rather warm, grew to be *very* warm, and at last unendurably hot and stuffy, until, half choked, and tormented into the bargain by the stalks of hay, which tickled her face, she determined to change her attitude, so as to lie with her head towards the opening and her feet the other way.

Upon attempting to execute this manœuvre, what was her horror to discover that it was absolutely impossible for her to do anything of the sort ! In vain she tried to work her shoulders round, almost breaking her neck in two in the effort ; the closely-packed hay held her like a vice, and absolutely forbade advance in any direction, save one, namely straight forward into the stack, which would, of course, have the result of leading her further and further away from the light and safety which was to be found at the entrance.

The sympathetic reader may easily imagine the agony which now possessed our unfortunate adventuress ! This time it was no imaginary peril either, but a very real one—so real that for years afterwards, she has owned to me, she was in the habit of waking up at night, believing that she was once more in the stack, and was once more undergoing the shock and horror of that first discovery ! In vain she next tried to back out. This movement, like the first, proved to be absolutely impossible. Had there been any one outside it might have been done, but to extricate herself in this fashion unaided, was, she soon discovered, out of question.

Terror had by this time reached a point where reason almost gave way. Voices sounded in her ears—terrible voices, roaring out half-heard but horrible messages. There were moments when the whole situation seemed to her

to be unreal ; moments when it seemed as if it
were to some one else—some one whom she had
read about in a story—rather than to herself,
that this dreadful thing had happened.   And
again the next minute, like a flood, it would
rush back across her mind that it was nothing
of the sort ; that it was to no bloodless child of
fiction, but to herself, her own very self, that it
had happened ; that *she*, and no one else, was
shut up in this dreadful, living, hay-made tomb.

Nightmare followed nightmare.   A vision of
the haystack being opened long afterwards, and
a skeleton—her own skeleton—being found in
it, as she had once found the skeleton of a frog
in a dried-up tank, rose for a moment before
her brain.   The hay too !   There was something so treacherous, so horrible in the idea of
the hay—the friendly, well-beloved hay, with
which she and the others had played ten thousand times, whose very smell had an endearing
flavour—that *it*, of all things, should have
turned into her destroyer !

Wild with terror, she next began twisting
herself over and over, backwards and forwards
as far as the limits of her burrow would allow,
hurting and bruising herself badly in her agon-
ized efforts to escape.   She tried to scream, but
the hay seemed to absorb her voice, so that it

grew choked, and lost before any sound could penetrate to the outside. Exhausted at last by these efforts, she lay like a dead creature, almost believing by moments that she *was* dead ; almost glad that she was, that so, at least, this horrible business might be over and done with.

No one, however, least of all no one at ten years old, succumbs to disaster without a second, a third, and a fourth effort. Presently the idea came to our prisoner, that since she could not turn round, and so escape by the way she had come in, she had better perhaps push on in the direction in which she lay, and try if she could not reach the other side. A new horror, however, suddenly presented itself. What if the passage never *did* reach the other side ? What if it came to an end in the middle of the stack ? In that case she would merely have lost the one hope of being extricated, which she still retained.

Sickening as this idea was, it had to be faced, and summoning all her courage, she made a resolute effort to move onward. Little by little, an inch at a time, digging a trough for herself with her hands as she went on, and dragging her body through it, she advanced slowly and laboriously, like some small mole, or other terrestrial digger. At any moment the hay might come upon her from above, and then indeed there would be an end of all things. Meantime, it had not yet come down, and she was certainly making some way.

When, with great difficulty and innumerable delays, she had traversed about two-thirds of the stack, a faint ray of light, a partial mitigation of the darkness in which she had hitherto lain, began to penetrate to her from the outer world. Hope, nearly dead, sprang up again in her breast, and she was upon the point of thinking that after all she might perhaps make her own way out unaided, when she was once more brought up short by a new obstacle, this time by a huge beam of wood which, running right across the middle of the stack, made it impossible for her to advance a single inch further.

It was this beam which had, no doubt, kept the passage open. At the same time, it now put a stop to all further advance, for even had she been able to move it, it was clear that the hay would simply in that case have closed in on her. All that she could do was to creep as close to it as she dared, and stretching out her hands, draw any hay she could get hold of towards her, tucking it away under her body, so as by that means to open the passage and let in a little more light. Beyond this there was nothing to be done but to wait, in the hope that sooner or later some one would pass by, who would hear her if she called.

At last—how long after her imprisonment began I cannot say, but to herself it seemed many days—there did reach her ears the sound of voices, not phantom ones this time, but genuine human voices, the voices of two of the workmen talking together somewhere near the cowhouse.

A flood of hope broke over her brain, and lifting herself as much as she could, she shouted again and again, stretching out her hands frantically towards the entrance. For some time she failed to attract their attention. Happily, one of the men had occasion to pass between the stack and the cowhouse, and hearing his step approaching, she again uttered a piercing shriek, and this time there was no doubt that the man heard, for she could hear his responsive roar of terror and dismay, as, throwing down the pitchfork which he held in his hands, he fled for his life.

Had it been the middle of the night probably nobody would have ventured again to approach that bewitched haystack. Happily in broad daylight curiosity after a time overcame superstition, for the steps presently returned, and

after a good deal more delay, and a good deal
more suspense on the part of the prisoner, she
was able to make them understand that it was
no "pooka," no "clurigan," but a living person
—herself, in short—who was calling to them
from the inside of the stack.

Even when this had at last been made clear,
and when two stout pairs of arms had been set
to work to liberate her, it took a considerable
time and nearly the total demolition of the haystack before that deliverance could be accomplished.   But when at last it *was* accomplished;
when, after that dreadful term of incarceration,
her feet once more touched solid earth ; when
she could again breathe and see with comfort ;
then, ah then, what a lovely world it was that
burst upon her view !   What a glory lay upon
every blade of grass ; what beauty, as of heaven
itself, bathed the stones, the tree trunks, the
cowhouse, the very muck-heaps !   No Dante
fresh from visiting his Inferno, no Milton newly
"escaped the Stygian night, through utter and
through middle darkness borne," ever revisited
the light, or felt "its vital sovereign lamp"
with a more complete, a more absolute sense of
beatitude.   And when, turning away from this
scene of her miseries, she began to retrace her
steps towards the house, and could see it shining

D

ahead of her through the trees—*the* house, the
House of Houses, the Beloved one—how different did it look from that stony aspect of it
which had met her eyes in the early dawn!
What pitying glances, on the contrary, did it
seem now to be bestowing upon her!   How it
stretched out its arms towards its truant, who
had been in such deadly peril since they last
enclosed her!   How all its open windows and
doors seemed to be calling to her, and how,
as she ran sobbing along the path, her own
heart yearned, and thrilled, and leaped towards
it in return!

It was not until hours after all this; not
until our repentant wanderer had been received,
scolded, questioned, finally kissed, and comforted; not till she had had some hours of
much-needed sleep in her own bed under the
pink quilt; not till after all this excitement
was at an end, that, for the first time since the
early morning, she suddenly remembered her
capture, that capture which was to make her
name famous for ever!   Springing from her
bed, she ran quickly to where her jacket had
been thrown, and plunged her hand with beating heart into its pocket.   Alas! in her many
writhings and wrigglings the chip box had long
since resolved itself into a mere handful of

broken chips, while of the captive itself—the "Great Unknown," the "New to Science," the first, the only one of the sort that she in her life ever beheld—it had resolved itself into a few pinches of vividly green dust at the very bottom of her pocket!

ON THE PURSUIT OF MARINE ZOOLOGY AS AN INCENTIVE TO GOSSIP

I HAVE sometimes flattered myself, when temporarily established in some more than usually out-of-the-way spot — an Atlantic-scourged lodging let us say, or the outworks of a lighthouse, or some such picturesque locality—that I could get on without any one to cook for me. It was an exhilarating dream, and I have even gone so far as to try once or twice to reduce it to practical experience, but must own that the plan is not one that I can conscientiously recommend for general adoption. Self-made stir-about is indigestible, unless stirred for a longer period than impromptu cooks are wont to bestow upon it. Bacon, fried over a sitting-room fire, is apt to leave more permanent reminiscences of its presence than one would think possible, while a prolonged course of tinned soups and potted meats has other results needless to particularize. If, worn out with these amateur efforts, one hastily summons some local assistant to one's aid, no amount of patriotism—I am speaking of Ireland—will enable me to assert that one invariably finds even an embryo Francatelli ready to one's hand. This confession will explain why it is that I cherish such a special sentiment of gratitude towards my good friend Mrs. O'Donnell, who upon more than one occasion has advanced gallantly to the rescue, when, having rashly thrust myself into some such situation as those indicated above, I was suffering from the natural consequences.

Herself a native of the west of Ireland, Mrs. O'Donnell is well acquainted with its capabilities, and what is even more important, with its limitations. Her own native region is not, however, either Clare or Galway, which were my two chief haunts at that time, but Roscommon, where, according to her own account, she had always lived " with the very heighth of quality." I think she must have done so, for her conversation showed exactly the blending which comes of a more or less conscious copying of the talk of one's nominal superiors, grafted on to a native vocabulary of immeasurably greater vigour and picturesqueness.

She was an excellent cook, but her talk was better than even her "made dishes," and our morning dialogues—ostensibly upon the subject of ducks and chickens—were apt to stray to a greater distance from those topics than would be believed by any one who has not realized from what insignificant starting-points the conversation of two really intelligent and sympathetic people will in time diverge.

After this last remark, which has a flavour about it of vainglory, I had better hasten to add that my own share of these dialogues was all but entirely negative, being limited to a preliminary question, with perhaps an appropriate interjection thrown in now and then, whenever the stream of Mrs. O'Donnell's eloquence showed some symptoms of abating.

Confidences are so enticing that, once begun, it is difficult to leave them off, however little flattering they may be to the confider's vanity. I had better therefore confess that a deep and entirely self-interested design lay at the base of the apparent carelessness with which I was in the habit of alluring Mrs. O'Donnell into the stream of her professional reminiscences. Although her good-will toward me had few limits, there was one point upon which she more than once frankly told me that I was really too great a trial to be put up with. That point was as follows. Close to my door, and still closer to hers—the kitchen door—lay on more than one of these occasions the shingly shore of that long sea-loch known as the Greater Killary, upon whose southern bank I was the happy temporary owner of a cottage. To dredge in those friendly, and not too perturbing waters ; to extract from them every wriggling, writhing, prickly, slimy, glassy, brittle-rayed, tentacle-armed, spine-protected, or weed-resembling creature that their depths afforded, was at that date not merely the main occupation of my life, but its serious, though, I need hardly say, entirely self-appointed, business and avocation.

Brought to the shore in pails and buckets, where were receptacles to be found in which my captures, possibly discoveries, could be bestowed ? Only one hunting-ground for such receptacles lay within reach, and that one— alas, poor Mrs. O'Donnell !—was the kitchen. Jars, jam-pots, milk-pans—comparatively venial thefts—being quickly exhausted, the votary of marine zoology next laid felonious hands upon the very arcana of the place, upon pie-dishes,

upon salad-bowls, upon—shall I, dare I confess
it?—frying-pans, fish-pans and stew-pans, so
long that is to say as they were the "best"
ones, for the viler, unlined, and therefore
readily corroding ones were perfectly safe
from such assaults.

These depredations being of almost daily
occurrence, it will be seen how necessary
it became to find also some daily topic upon
which to divert conversation when the stream
of Mrs. O'Donnell's eloquence seemed likely
to descend in all its native vigour upon the
marauder's head. Like other habitual criminals
I grew excessively cunning, and soon discovered
that to turn that eloquence rapidly upon the
sayings and doings of her previous employers
was the only way of averting it from myself
and my delinquencies. In this manner I
unintentionally acquired a good deal of rather
miscellaneous information about the various
families which had at different times had the
advantage of Mrs. O'Donnell's services. It
was an odd result of a prolonged and con-
scientious series of zoological investigations, but
I am afraid that it was the only one which
permanently resulted from it!

Of these families the chief was the now
rather embarrassed family of the Carrowmores,

upon whose estate Mrs. O'Donnell had been born, in whose kitchen she had graduated, and in whose affairs she took the deepest and most affectionate interest. With me her theme was chiefly the last Lord Carrowmore, although from her account he seems to have been rather a degenerate member of a well-known and stalwart house. Indeed Mrs. O'Donnell's whole tone in speaking of him presented an odd mixture of awe for what he represented, combined with a sort of regretful pity for what as a matter-of-fact he himself was. I give her narrative as nearly as possible as it reached me, omitting a few irrelevancies.

A SONG OF "VEILED REBELLION"

THEY say that grave perils surround me,
  That foes are on every hand ;
That to right, and to left, and around me,
  Red murder is stalking the land.
        Yet I sit, as you see,
          'Neath the shade of a tree,
        With my book on my knee.

I am one of the demons accursed,
  Detested, denounced from of old ;
For whose blood the whole land is athirst,
  Or so I am credibly told.
        Yet I sit, as you see,
          'Neath the shade of a tree,
        With my book on my knee.

My safety is guarded all day
  By stalwart protectors in green,
Who roam with my maids thro' the hay,
  And happily rarely are seen.
        While I sit, as you see,
          'Neath the shade of a tree,
        With my book on my knee.

MRS. O'DONNELL'S REPORT

"In course you're aware, ma'am, they were always great people, the Carrowmores, the very top and glory of all the noble families of Roscommon," Mrs. O'Donnell would begin. "Thought a power of themselves, they did, and small wonder! Grand-looking ladies and gentlemen, every one of them! Why to see Mr. John George—that's the present lord—coming up the avenue of Castle Gaddery, with his chest tossed out, and he not looking at you, no, nor seeing you, no more than if you weren't in it at all—dear me, it was a pleasure! They were all like that; grand gentry, high-steppin' and proud, every one of them. A real out-and-out noble family. Dear me! dear me!

"What sort of a place was Castle Gaddery, ma'am? Dear heart! doesn't every one know that there's not its match in all Ireland, let alone the county of Roscommon! Why,

when the old lord and lady—that's *my* lord's
father and mother—was first married, 'twas
four horses they'd have out whenever they went
to take the air in the neighbourhood, so it was
—four horses, yes, indeed, not a horse less!
That was before my time, but 'twas always the
same, always.   Why, when the railway was first
opened to Athlone, I've heard say her old ladyship could not be got to step into the train, no
nor to look at it, 'cept she might sit in her own
coach the whole time!   Yes, indeed, and sit in
it she did, too, till the day of her death, till the
day of her death, did her old ladyship!   Oh, a
grand family they were always, and a grand
house, and a grand place, and grand ways
entirely!

"Too much grandeur is it, ma'am?   Well,
may be so, indeed, the way the property is
now.   Still, rich or poor, they were always
like that; always great and respected.   Held
their heads high, higher than any one else in
the county; young and old, first and last, all
the same, none like them far or near; all, that
is, but the last one—*my* lord, as I always
called him, having lived with him so long.
He was never like a real Carrowmore at all,
so he was not, poor dear, kind gentleman;
quite a different sort entirely!   Small and thin

in the body, a trifling-looking man to be one
of *that* stock. A dark skin he had, with a
narrow sort of a face, and only a small bit of
a black moustache on his upper lip, whereas
the Carrowmores, every one of them, were
fair men, with beautiful grand beards on their
chins as they got on in life. Beautiful,
indeed, beautiful!"

Mrs. O'Donnell would pause and sigh, stroking
her own chin down with an air of contemplation.

"Maybe his looks wouldn't have mattered so
much, only that it was his *ways*, too, you see,
ma'am, that were different; not like *that* family's
ways at all, at all! How he come to be so different I never could think; but it was a pity, a
great pity! From the time he was a boy he
was always the same; coshering round with the
poor people for one thing, and listening to their
foolish talk; that and wandering about by
himself, or sitting up half the night to read
books—as common-looking books as ever you
saw in your life; not like a lord's books at all,
so they wer'n't. Writing away for hours too at
a time he'd be, so that any one 'd think it was
paid he was for doing it. I understand as
often as not 'twould be poetry he'd be writing.
Poetry! to think of that! My God! and he
a Carrowmore! Poor dear gentleman! poor

dear gentleman ! He was as kind a man as ever
lived, and a good master, too, but it was a
sad trouble to the family.

"Did *I* ever read any of his poetry,
ma'am ! No, indeed, what would ail me to be
reading it? Terrible indeed, terrible! Still, I
always maintain he was a well-meaning gentleman, and so I'll say to the day of my death,
let who will be there. He might be a bit
foolish in some things, but he had the nicest,
easiest ways ever *I* knew in a gentleman ; yes,
and a sharp tongue he had, too, in his head, had
me lord, mind you, when he chose. Oh, yes,
ma'am ; there was none durst take a liberty with
him, simple as he seemed, so there was not.
Generous? 'deed, you *may* say that ! he *was*
generous—why he would give the very coat off
his back, or the shoes off his feet, so he would,
and not look to see if he was thanked either,
though 'twas terrible poor he was himself,—
that is, for a Carrowmore,—and he the eldest
of all. 'Twasn't at his own place, Castle
Gaddery, he lived, you understand, in those
days I'm speaking of, ma'am. 'Twas only
in a small little house six miles, or maybe
seven miles, below Shannon-bridge ; a house no
bigger than this one, if as big. His own
house, Castle Gaddery, had been shut up ever

since the old lord died.   Why, the roof of it
alone cost more, I'm told, to keep up than *my*
lord, God help him, had to live on in the year.
However, that didn't seem to matter to him.
He was always that simple and natural, I
believe, if you'll credit me, he liked a small
house best, so he did !   It was in and out, in
and out of doors with him the whole day long.
Sometimes he'd be wandering along by the river-
bank, or sitting writing up in an old Dane's
Fort of a place there was at the back beyont.
Then indoors again, playing a bit of a tune
maybe on the piany, and with that out again,
over and over again.   As often as not he'd be
doing nothing, only sitting and staring at the
sky, or the trees, and smiling to himself !
Foolish ways ; 'deed yes, so they were, only *I*
never minded him, you see, being so used
to his goings-on.

"A large establishment !   Oh bless you, no,
ma'am ; there was only meself in the house,
and a couple of girls under me, and an old
man they called Phineas Ruddy, that had been
stable-helper in the old lord's time.   A fool he
was, if ever there was a fool born into this world,
was that Phineas Ruddy, God knows ; yes,
indeed, he *was* a fool, and worse than a fool.

"Didn't he have any of his relations with

him? Well no, not to say living with him, ma'am. You see the house was that ill-convenient, as one might say, being all doors and windows. Now and then some of his nephews and nieces would come for a bit— very kind it was of them, and a fine fuss his lordship would be in beforehand to make sure they had all they wanted. Now and then, too, he'd have a gentleman friend to stay with him, when nobody else was about—queer-looking gentlemen some of them were, the queerest ever *I* saw, with long hair, and the oddest made clothes. And talk, talk! dear help us, how those gentlemen did talk! Outlandish languages some of them, so they did, but *I* never minded. As sure as one of them would arrive, me lord would be more out of doors than ever, sailing down the river, or going into caves with candles, or walking about repeating poetry, and a power of such-like doings. Harmless? Well, yes, harmless in course, only queer, you know—more especially when you think of his being a Carrowmore !

"Well, ma'am, the troubled times come on after I'd been about six years with his lordship, and the whole country was turned upside down, what with meetings and speeches and seranadings up and down the world with tin pikes

and gold crowns, and harps dressed up in
green ribbons, and flags with 'Death to the
Tyrants' and 'Glory to Irin,' and the rest of
the goings-on!   There was a grand meeting
soon after it all began up at Ballinabarney, the
first ever there was in that part of the country,
and a number of speeches made by Parliament
gentlemen come down to it a purpose from
Dublin.   Grand speeches I'm told they were,
telling the people that they were not going to
be slaves no longer, and they so pleased to be
told it, the creatures, that you might have heard
them whooping, and screeching, and making the
devil's own diversion right away at our back
gate, which was more nor a mile from the place,
yes, indeed, more nor a mile.   I heard from one
that was at it, that me lord was specially spoke
of by name, as a 'blood-sucker,' and a 'di-
vourer of orphins,' and a 'coorooneted ghoul,'
because of Castle Gaddery, you know, being not
far off, ma'am, though it was little *he* ever got
out of it, as every one in the world knew, the
whole property being swallowed up with debts,
and mortgages, and the like.   I remember by
the same token as they were going home that
afternoon, a lot of young fellows stopped at the
cross roads, which was just below the house, and
hooted and screeched at the tops of their voices

E

'To Hell with Carrowmore,' and 'Three
cheers for the little Preghaun's buryin' !'

"What did they mean by Preghaun? Oh,
that was just a name they had for him because
of his being so black, and so small, you know.
Me lord heard them himself, for I saw him
standing outside the study window at the time,
with his head a one side, and he listening for
all the world as if he liked it, though I don't
suppose he rightly could.

"Well, ma'am, me lord's nephews and nieces
they didn't come over at all, at all, that year to
stop with him, leastways none of his nieces did,
and I misremember that any of his nephews did
'cept it was Mr. Algernon—that's Mr. John
George's—I mean the present lord's eldest son.
He came for a short time at the beginning of
the troubles, and there was great talk between
him and me lord, and Mr. Clancy, the agent,
and I heard Mr. Algernon say there was nothing
like firmness, and that you oughtn't to give
way, not if it was ever so. You'll wonder
how I heard, but I was putting by some of the
chimbley ornaments, as it happened that afternoon, in a closet which was convenient to the
study, so I heard a good deal of what went
on. Mr. John George, it seems, wrote the
same thing from London, and very displeased

he was with me lord, I heard, for being so weak and easy-going, giving way at every turn, and letting the property be destroyed and rejuced in his hands, he having, as Mr. John George told him, only a life use of it, so that it was his duty to remember those that came after him, and not to let the rents be cut down and rejuced the way they were. Well, ma'am, after all their talking, Mr. Algernon he went off to London by the early train, and me lord he just stayed on by himself, and in and out and about with him, the same as usual, not appearing to notice anything that was going on. That was one of the queer things about him. To see him you'd never believe anything was happening in the country, no more than if Mr. Parnell, and Mr. Davitt, and the rest of the Parliament gentlemen had never been born nor heard of !

"Didn't he read the papers and learn what was happening that way ? Well, if you'll take my word for it, ma'am, I don't believe he did, or as good as never. There was no Dublin paper, or Cork, or Limerick paper come to him to my certain knowledge the whole time I was in the house, and only one London one—I misremember what the name of it was now——"

"*The Times?*"

"Oh, no, ma'am, I shouldn't have mis-remembered *that* name on account of its being all but the same, you may say, as the *Irish Times;* 'twas a much smaller paper whatever its name was. Anyway he had that, and a couple more that used to come to him every week. Their names began with an *A*, both of them, that I'm sure of, for I had to open and iron them out by the kitchen fire. Those he'd read, but as for the other, as often as not it would be lying uncut day after day till I'd ask his lordship if I might take it to top the jam-pots with. 'Certainly, Mrs. O'Donnell; to be sure, my good Mrs. O'Donnell,' he'd say, not knowing what I was saying to him, the creature, no more than if it was Greek I was talking, but smiling up at me with that look he had in his eyes when he was thinking of something else : very aggravating some people thought it, only *I* didn't mind, being so used, you see, to his ways.

"One thing there was I couldn't get used to though, and that was the way he would sit the whole day long with the windows open, and the blinds pulled up to the very top; yes, indeed, all day, ma'am, and half the night too, often! Dreadful it was to see, remembering the bad work that was going on about in the country; as every one else in the world knew if *he* didn't.

"'Hadn't you better let me shut down that window, me lord?' I'd say to him, coming in from the kitchen, and he maybe standing there with a candle in his hand, looking at the books in the book-case, or else walking up and down the room, and as plain to be seen, though he was but a small gentleman, as a bluebottle fly on a gas-lamp! Tempting Providence, it was, no better! for none could tell who mightn't be outside there in the dark, convenient in the bushes, and only waiting and watching on the sly till they could get him easiest, and be off before e'er a one could touch them.

"However, I might as well have talked to an old image that he kept on the shelf for anything he minded. 'What's that, Mrs. O'Donnell?'' he'd say, looking round at me in a sort of half-awake way, so that I'd know that he didn't hear or heed, the creature, what was being said to him, though always, I will say, as civil as civil. 'Shut down the window?' he'd say then. 'Oh, dear, no, Mrs. O'Donnell, 'tis an enchanting evening, and I'm just waiting for the moon to rise, and then I'll go for a little stroll along the river, so you needn't hurry about dinner. And, if I'm not back in time, you can just put it by for me, Mrs. O'Donnell,' that's what his lordship would say, reaching down for his hat, which he kept on a peg near the window. Indeed, 'twas but a morsel he'd eat at the best of times, ma'am, scarce enough to keep the life in a crow, and as often as not he'd take that little out with him in his pocket, and eat it anywhere, on the roadside just like a tramp, or in the boat on the river, or oftenest of all in that old place he was so fond of going to, the Seven Churches they call it, you know, ma'am. 'Twas a curious thing, and a thing I often remarked, for all he was such a delicate gentleman he seemed able to be more out of doors than any one *I* ever saw, let alone a lord. Indeed, even when he was in the house, it would be in and out with him, often long after every one else was in bed, so it would, extraordinary !

"Well, ma'am, I'd just have to go back to the kitchen, which was nearly opposite— as it might be across that passage there— and sit down, and try to keep myself quiet, though it was uneasy enough I was in my mind, as I well might be, God knows.

"Police protection ? Oh, no, ma'am, that

was a thing his lordship never would hear
of, not if it was ever so ; and, though he was
such an easy gentleman, he wasn't one you would
make have a thing if his mind was set against
it, so he was not. At the beginning of the
troubles the Government did send a sergeant
and two polis—big, upstanding men they were,
any of them would have made six of me lord
—and wrote to him, so I understood, that
they was to stop in the house, and to follow
him about wherever he went, as a sure word
had gone up to Dublin Castle that his name
was down in the black list, and that he was
to be shot. Me lord was too civil to send
them away at the first, and told me to see
that they had plenty to eat, and as much whisky
as they liked, only for God's sake to keep
them out of his sight. Indeed, a pair of
quieter young fellows than the two polis
couldn't be seen ; decent, easy-going boys ; give
them what food and drink they wanted, 'twas
all they asked. But the sergeant he was a
black, sour-looking Orangeman from the north,
and a different sort altogether. Stiff in his
ways he was, very stiff, as all them Orangemen
are. 'Does your lordship propose attendin'
divine service to-morrow afternoon ?' says he
the first day they come—which, as it happened,

was a Saturday—and he standing up stiff and straight in the passage, which was so narrow that there was scarce room for the shoulders of him in it. Now me lord was not greatly given to attendin' service, morning or afternoon, and that's the truth, being fonder of wandering about, and reading his own books, and the likes of that. Anyway, he couldn't stand being asked no such questions, no, nor being followed about, nor stared at, not being used to it, and howsoever he managed it, he stopped the Government from sending any more polis, and from that day on he just went in and out in his own way, with the windows always wide open, and he inside playing on the piany, as much as to tell the people where they'd find him, and giving no more heed to himself than if he'd been safe in the middle of Merrion Square !

"Well, ma'am——" here Mrs. O'Donnell made a long pause, and heaved another deep sigh. "Well, ma'am, it come at last ! One day—a Thursday it was I remember, for I'd been speaking to the woman that used to hawk fish round from Athlone—a cheat she was, born and bred, if ever there was one in *this* world—Anastasia Doolin was her name, and her husband's was Mick McGeoghelan,

that had one of the boats on the river, a
thieving, ill-tongued pair, the two of them,
as any in Roscommon ! Well, ma'am, I had
been buying some mackerel from her for the
next day's dinner for ourselves, and a couple
over that would do, said I, for me lord !

"'Och ! Glory, glory ! Great Queen of
glory ! how mighty grand we are with our
lords !' says she, sneering like, though there
was black rage all the time, as I knew well, in
her heart, along of my having found out that
she'd sold me a white sole in the place of a
black one, only the last Friday was a fortnight.

"' Take care of that fine lord of yours, Mrs.
O'Donnell, ma'am ! take care of him !' says
she, threatening me with her finger. 'Keep a
bit of a cord about his legs, and don't let him out
of your sight, that grand lord, for feard you
might lose him ! Make the most of him with
your pride and your grandeur, boasting it up
and down the country that you're serving a lord,
though it *is* the smallest and the meanest-look-
ing lord ever was seen, no bigger than a jack-
snipe, and that would have been put out of it
long before this if he'd only been a reasonable-
sized man, instead of a poor *pitiogue* that the
boys can hardly see, and might be shooting at

him all day and night too without hitting him,
so they might, the darlin's.'

"'What's that, woman? What wickedness
are you saying?' screams I.

"'Woman, indeed! woman yourself!' says
she, with a toss of her head. 'Take care, I
tell you, of that fine lord of yours, for by the
piper that played before Moses 'twon't be
many days longer you'll be able to boast of how
you're serving a lord, so it won't!' And with
that off with her, and not another word, good
or bad, could I get from her.

" Well, ma'am, if I was oneasy before, you
may think 'twas twice as oneasy I was then, for
those hawking people do hear everything that's
said in the country, good or bad. So I asked
Phineas Ruddy to find out, if he could, what
was going on at all, at all. And he asked one, and
he asked another, and at last he found out that
there was great talk of how Phil Foggarty had
sworn at the 'Heart of Irin,' that he'd do for me
lord within three months, on account of a farm
over at Castle Gaddery, that Mr. Clancy, the
agent, had taken from one of the Foggartys.
Now it wasn't *Phil* Foggarty's farm at all, as
it happened, no, nor belonging to any of
his family, but to *Luke* Foggarty, that had
been paid off six months before, and gone to

America, and was only Phil's second cousin at the best, even when he was in it. What business had he to go taking up other people's business and putting himself to the fore, I should like to know, and he not even asked?—such interferin' ways!

"Well, ma'am, the time went on, and no more about it, so I began to hope nothing would happen, more particular as no one had had sight or sound latterly of Phil Foggarty in the country. However, one evening towards the end of September, I was dishing up the dinner, when I heard the sound of a shot coming from the little wood just beyond me lord's study. Well, when I heard that, the dish I had in my hands leaped clean out of them, with the terror I was in, and broke to bits on the floor, and I screeched to Phineas Ruddy to run and see what had happened. But he pretended not to hear, though he heard me right well, the old bogart. With that I gathered myself up, and I run to the study, but before I could get there, Bang! Bang! went that gun again, and when I got to the room there was a cloud of smoke in it, enough to blind you, and a queer smell too, like pepper, that set me sneezing. Well, when I had got the water a bit out of my eyes, I looked round for me lord. And if you'll

believe me, ma'am, he was sitting in his chair
for all the world as if nothing had happened,
only the book he had been reading at the time
fallen over on the floor, as it might be there at
your feet, and the window open as usual down
to the ground, and the smoke hanging about
him, so that I could scarce see him at first in
the middle of it.

"'My God, me lord!' screams I. 'My
God, me lord, what is it?' says I. 'Don't
tell me you're hit,' says I.

"'Really, Mrs. O'Donnell,' says he, 'really,
my good Mrs. O'Donnell, I'm not very sure
about it yet myself,' says he. And with that
he puts up his hand to his shoulder, and 'I
believe, now you mention it, I am,' says he.

"Well, at that I ran to him, ma'am, as you
may believe, and looked at his shoulder, and,
sure enough, there was blood staining the back
of his coat, for he was sitting with his back to
the window at the time. It didn't seem much
of a wound, though, for all that amount of
shooting and smoke and noise. It wasn't low
down either, only right up at the top of his
shoulder. For all that, the moment I caught
sight of the blood I let a screech, and began
crying thieves and fire and murder, and with
that Phineas Ruddy ran into the room with a

big old gun, he had got hidden somewhere, loose in his hands, and his face as white as that sheet of paper before you, ma'am, and he all shake-shaking, so that it was plain to see he couldn't hold it straight, much less shoot with it, the creature.

" 'Give me that gun,' says his lordship, speaking a bit sharp, but keeping quite still, only his eyes opening wider than ever I seen them open before, and he looking at a spot in a big clump of fuchey bushes there was outside, where we could see something moving, now that the smoke was beginning to clear away.

" With that he upped with the gun to his shoulder, though I could see by the twitch of his face it hurt him bad to lift it, and let blaze into the middle of that fuchey bush. Well, ma'am, at that there comes a great roaring and screeching out of the clump, so that I made sure in my own mind it was one of them polis, the creatures, that had come up hearing the shot, or a pig, maybe, rootin' there, for I didn't think it could be any one else. But, no ! if you'll believe me, it was Phil Foggarty himself and no other, though what made him stop after he'd done his job nobody ever could guess. Anyhow, there he was, and tumbled out on to the gravel, he did, bleeding, and roaring, and crying he was murdered, and his own gun smoking hot all the time in his hands! I suppose he thought he might as well stop and see the end of it, because of there being only us three women in the house, and Phineas Ruddy that was little better, and no one in the world believing that me lord, who was always so easy-going, would shoot back, let it be ever so. However, shoot back he did, ma'am, for I saw it with my own eyes, just as I'm telling you, and when the polis came up, which they did in about an hour's time, they'd nothing to do but to take Phil Foggarty off with them on a car to Athlone, and into the jail with him there as easy as easy.

"Was me lord badly hurt? Well, not so very badly, ma'am, still he had to go to bed, and Phineas Ruddy was sent off post-haste to Ballynahoola for the doctor, though it was three in the morning by the same token before he could bring him back, on account of two other men having been hit that same night not far from Lucknadarrah, and he sent for to cut the bullets out of them. There was no bullet to be cut out of me lord, praise be to God, only a bit of a flesh wound at the top of his shoulder, and another in the calf of his leg that we hadn't found out at first, and a shock, so the doctor said, to the whole inside of him. But, if he'd keep quiet, and eat all he could, he'd be as well as ever in a week, so the doctor told him, or a month at the very most.

"Howsomever, it was coming on cold weather then, the beginning of October, and me lord had to lie on the sofey the whole day, 'stead of trapesing over the country the way he was used. It was an early winter, too, that year, and wet, very wet. You could hear the rain pattering from every part of the house, so that it got quite distressful, and I suppose he was moped listening to it. He used to lie there with his books about him, and now and then he'd read a little bit out of one of them, and a little bit out of another, but most times he'd be just looking out at the window, and humming a bit of a tune to himself; a dreary tune it was to listen to, and one that give me the melancholies to hear, for I would be in and out of that study room of his all day long, you'll understand, ma'am, bringing him his beef-tea, or a drop of mulled wine, or anything else I thought he'd take. 'Twas little enough, God knows. He was always a poor eater, but from that time forward he eat less and less every day, less and less, so he did, less and less!" Here Mrs. O'Donnell's apron

went up to her eyes, and she began to sob gently.
" A poor eater always, the poorest ever *I* knew
for a gentleman ; but after that time 'twould
have broken any one's heart to be cooking for
him, and see the food coming back day after day
scarce touched, only a bit of vegetable, maybe,
or a drop of gravy, nothing else, though he'd
stir about the things on his plate, so he would,
making believe he was eating a power—he was
always thoughtful, was his poor lordship.   At
last, ma'am, seeing him so moped, what with
eating so little, and having no company, I made
bold to write myself to London to Mr. John
George, though I was never a fine writer, as
you know, nor much of a scholard at the best of
times.   Still I made shift to tell him that some
one ought, I thought, to come over and see to
me lord, who was looking badly. 'Deed, 'twas a
pitiful sight to see him getting smaller and
smaller every day he lived, and the eyes of him
bigger and bigger, so that it was no solider than
a half-grown tom-tit he'd look, lying on that
sofey of his, smothered in big books, and not
able to read them either, for I'd see him lift
first one and lay it down, and then another,
dropping them back with a sort of a sigh.   Not
that they would have done him any good if he
had been able to read them, in course, for what

good could books do any gentleman, least of all a sick one?

"Did Mr. John George come, ma'am? 'Deed he did, and beautiful he looked with that great beard of his, beautiful. But if you'll believe me, often and often afterwards, though it seems a strange thing to say, I was a'most sorry in my own mind I'd ever written to him, so I was. You see, ma'am, Mr. John George he was a regular Carrowmore—a grand-looking gentleman, always busy and important like—a wonderful determined man, as everybody said, and the best head for business out and out anywhere. As for health, I don't suppose he'd ever had an ache nor a pain in his life, unless it was, maybe, the toothache, or a bit of the indigestion when he'd eaten his dinner too fast. Now me lord he was always ailing and delicate, always, from the time he was a boy. It didn't need Phil Foggarty to be shooting him, the blackguard, to make him delicate, though I don't suppose that did him any good either; inside or out.

"Dear me, ma'am, to see those two gentlemen together it was a curiosity, a regular curiosity, remembering that they was brothers. Mr. John George—I mean his present lordship, I do be always callin' him wrong—would stand

F

over against the fireplace, looking so grand and
tall, and his beard all fluffed out splendid, telling me lord that he ought to do this, and that
he'd be quite well if he'd only do that. And me
lord he would just lie on the sofey, and look up
at him with those big eyes of his shining in his
wizendy little face ; and now and then he'd nod
his head, and say, 'Very likely, John,' or,
'Quite true, John,' only with a look all the
time in the corner of his eye, so that I could
see in his heart he wished his brother anywhere
on God's earth if he would only just go away
and leave him to himself. However, 'twas himself that had to go away in the end, for Mr.
John George said he couldn't stop longer in it,
and wouldn't go, not a step of him, till his
lordship agreed to go too ; which he did at
the last, though ill he liked it, as any one
could see. Indeed it was plain to me that he
intended to give Mr. John George the slip,
and come quietly back unbeknownst, for
one of the last words he said to me was,
'Don't forget that receipt of yours for the
stuffed tomatees, Mrs. O'Donnell,' says he. He
was always mighty partial to stuffed tomatees,
was his poor lordship, although such a poor
eater."

Mrs. O'Donnell's apron travelled slowly up

to her eyes, and again she sobbed softly to herself.

"Howsomdever, ma'am, he never did come back, neither for the stuffed tomatees, nor for nothing else, for they took him abroad to some foreign town—I misremember the name of it now, but I think it was in the south of Italy.

"Naples? Oh, no, ma'am, a longer name than that—four syllables there was to it to the best of my recollection—and about five months afterwards we heard that he'd got much worse, very bad indeed, and not likely to live. Whether it was the shooting, and the wound not healing rightly; or whether it was just the botheration of the whole thing, and being put out of his own easy ways; or whether it was the queer foreign food he would be getting in those onnatural places, or whatever it was, God knows. Anyway, he seems never to have done a bit of good, and every time we heard of him 'twas worse he was than the time before, and the next time would be worse still, till at last there come the very worst news of all. Yes indeed, he was dead, was his poor lordship, and buried, too, for they buried him out there in that foreign place he died in— Curious how I misremember its name, often as I have heard it ! But I had always a poor memory for names, 'cept it was the names of made dishes.

" Why didn't they bring him back to be buried at home, ma'am ? 'Deed, you may well ask *that*, and greatly talked of it was in the country, greatly talked of, and greatly wondered at ! Mr. John George—I mean his present lordship—gave out that it was along of the state of the neighbourhood, and that he didn't want his brother's corpse to be insulted, and it going to its burying. Maybe that *was* his reason, but for my part I never believed such a thing, so I did not. They was hard enough, and bad enough, and ondacent enough, God knows, those times ; still there was a power of people up and down the country that liked the poor lord right well, and would have gone a long way to see him laid in the ground decent, not to speak of hooting him, or the likes of that. Poor he might be, and small, not much to look at, and queer in his ways, not like a Carrowmore in the least, still he was a real gentleman when all was said, and a kind master, and so I'll maintain to my dying day. A good heart he had, too, the best heart in the world, though he *was* such a poor eater. Is it a duck or a

chicken I'll be ordering for you to-day, ma'am ?
There was a lot of fine young pullets running
round at Alicia O'Slatterly's last Sunday was a
week.   They ought to be coming on now, I
think ; nice tender eating."

OLD LORD KILCONNELL

WE had been sauntering for more than an
hour upon the terrace, with the tide the
while flowing in, and rapidly filling up all the
sinuosities of the little channel, each small
wave as it entered, spreading itself out, like
the train of a comet, getting thinner and
thinner, until recruited by a fresh rush of
salt water, which swept round the corner of
the nearest headland, on and on; up, up, up,
over the rocks, and sand, and slush, until, its
impetus exhausted, it died away in gasps and
murmurs amongst the grasses and sedums at
our feet.

We had been talking about—really I hardly
now remember what—our own affairs, I think,
and especially other people's; about the dreadful condition of the country—a most fertile
parent of illimitable platitudes !—about the

proper management of children; about the
right treatment and bringing up of Tigrinias
and Begonias. Across these improving topics
the twilight seemed somehow to keep stealing,
and to rob our remarks of half their natural
flatness. We lowered our voices now and
then, in the instinctive way people do when
something remote from themselves, something
a trifle larger, and a trifle less futile, seems
to lift a finger reprovingly for a minute in
the face of their respectable tittle-tattle.

Queenstown Bay, upon which we were then
gazing, is an excellent looking-glass upon which
to read the history of whatever movements
may chance at the moment to be going on in
the country overhead. Just then that country
seemed to have turned itself into the likeness
of a prodigious flower-garden, abloom with indescribable tints; abloom too with cloud-
flowers, unnamed by mortals, but no doubt
duly labelled and catalogued by their own
celestial gardeners.

My hostess's flower-garden, which lay a little
to the right of us, seemed almost worthy to be
the counterpart of this divine parterre, for it
was just then one blaze of autumn colouring,
a peculiar tawny orange predominating.

Every one, it is to be hoped, has heard of

the effects of South Cork climate upon horticulture, and this garden was a celebrated one
even in South Cork. Wonderful things grew,
and still grow in it. Eucalyptus and aloes;
cassias and yuccas; bignonias, making a glory
of lichen-covered walls; a jungle of bamboos
along the edge of a pool; palms or, at any
rate, palmettos; nay, in one sheltered nook, a
tree-fern, which had survived two winters,
although its fronds, I am bound to add, were
beginning when I last saw them to look a
little sorry for themselves. Up to the edge
of all this sub-tropical luxuriance the salt
waters of the bay came curling and crinkling
in, salting the grass, and leaving behind them
long streamers of oily-looking seaweeds, which
clung to the bank, and peered up in all directions upon the lawn. I used to wonder what
they and those fine acclimatized creatures in
the flower-beds thought of one another.

It was autumn—an Irish autumn at its best.
The sun shone all day with a mild and sleepy
benevolence upon the reluctant falling of the
leaves; upon the grass, touched already at the
summit with a trail of brown, but still fresh
and green below. Unlike the greater part
of Ireland, where the woods have been pared
to the very stump, the shores of Queens-

town Bay are fairly off for verdure. Immediately opposite to where we were walking, a house with ugly, ornamental chimneys showed upon a piece of rising ground; the "Great House" *par excellence* of the neighbourhood. Although as ugly as a house well could be, it was an imposing-looking structure in its way, backed as it was by a great sweep of woodland, and possessing two widely-spreading wings, linked to the main body by colonnades after a pseudo-classical fashion. In front of it extended a terrace, with vases ranged at intervals. Then the path suddenly narrowed, and dipped into a hollow amongst the trees, where it remained for some time invisible, re-emerging in the form of another terrace, which stretched for some distance along the shore, from which it was only divided by a balustrade, adorned at intervals with vases. I could hardly explain why, but the whole place seemed to me to have somehow taken on an air of decadence, almost of out-of-elbowness, since I saw it last. The woods looked rank; the vases, which at this season used to glow with geraniums, were empty; the windows of the house were shut, and only a barely-discernible thread of smoke rose languidly out of one of the great chimneys.

"Is Lord Kilconnell at home?" I presently inquired of my hostess.

"Yes, he is there," she answered, nodding her head in the direction of the channel. "He has been there the whole summer, but no one ever sees him. Poor man, it really *is* pitiful!" she went on after a moment. "He looks the mere ghost of what he was when you saw him last. He has never held up his head since Dermot Murrough died, and that is nearly four years ago. He just potters about the house and grounds, and has his dogs to keep him company; and goes round and looks at the eagles, and seals, and wombats, and the rest of the queer menagerie which poor Dermot brought together. That seems to be the only thing that gives him the slightest pleasure, which is all the more odd because he is not by way, you know, of having even yet forgiven Dermot."

"Let me see, what was it his son did?" I asked. "It was something rather bad, I remember, but the details seem to have escaped me."

"Oh, it's such a dreadfully melancholy subject. *Pray* don't let us talk about it," my hostess replied hastily.

Naturally I walked on again discreetly.

The tide was still steadily rising; the little ripples babbled and babbled; fussed discursively around all the stones; ran vehemently in shore, as if bent on conquering every green islet and headland within reach; finally dropped back, and contented themselves with a headlong scamper hither and thither amongst the sand and slush.

"Poor Dermot! *What* a pleasant creature he was! we shall *never* have so nice a neighbour again," my companion presently went on, as the most casual acquaintance with human nature must have convinced any one that she shortly would go on. "*Such* a contrast to that brother of his! It has always been a mystery to me how that tiresome priggish creature Saggart ever came to be his brother. Don't you think those Saggarts are the two greatest bores you ever met? And do you know, isn't it absurd? he— I mean Saggart—because his mother was an Englishwoman, always talks as though he were an Englishman himself. I am sure he safely might; no one would suspect him of being anything livelier. At the same time think of the absurdity of a man whose name, though he happens to be called Lord Saggart, is really Patrick

Murrough, declining to consider himself an Irishman!"

"Yes, but you've not told me about *Dermot* Murrough," I persisted, for I have no wish to be thought freer from the decent vice of curiosity than my neighbours, and I felt that I was being trifled with. "Let me see, he ran away with an actress, or something of that sort, and then married her?" I added, by way of helping matters on.

"An actress! Oh dear, no, it was nothing of *that* kind. It was much worse than that. It was with a girl here; with a girl belonging to their own property; that was the really terrible thing about it."

My companion stopped for a moment to disentangle a bramble which had caught in her skirt, after which she smoothed down the ruffled hem, glanced once more across the channel, and walked on beside me.

"Of course, he ought to have had a *profession*," she added, in that tone of rather comfortable retrospect with which people are in the habit of analyzing the causes of other people's failures. "Every young man ought to have a profession, especially every younger son. Somehow, though, with Dermot Murrough it didn't seem to matter so much as

with most younger sons. He was always so
lively. He was never bored or dull; it didn't
seem as if he *could* be bored if he had tried
to be. Everybody about here liked him so
much too; even the tenants were fond of him.
Yes, indeed, they really were! People always
laugh now-a-days if you say that the tenants
are fond of any of *us*. I don't say they are
often, but they *were* fond of Dermot Murrough. His not being the eldest son, and
having nothing therefore to say to the property, made everything easier, you know. He
and his father used to be here nearly the
whole year round at that time, and when Dermot was at home there was always something
amusing going on. He was for ever getting
up regattas for the fishermen, treats for the
labourers, teas for the women, bran pies for
the children; I don't know what all. He
used to offer prizes for the best pig, the best
rick of turf, the best jig-dancer, the best anything. He once offered a prize for the man
who would get first to the top of a hayrick
with his hands tied behind his back! His
father laughed, but let him do as he liked.
You remember that summer when you were
here last? Well, it was always just like that.
They were both of them devoted to yachting,

and used to make excursions together to all sorts of places, and bring the yacht back full of queer beasts and birds. Everything, in short, went well, until in an evil hour he fell in love with this girl, Mary Delaney."

"She was simply a peasant, you say?"

"Yes, the sister of a right-hand man of Dermot's, Phelim Delaney—you may remember him. He used to look after Dermot's hawks and eagles, and it was he who dug out that cavern at the bottom of the garden. He is there still, though I fancy it must be rather terrible for Lord Kilconnell to have to see him. This girl Mary was very handsome, and Dermot saw a great deal of her one summer, and got into the habit of walking about with her, and going out to meet her of an evening. He was dreadfully silly, poor dear, about women; always falling in love with some one in a head-over-heels sort of way. It had gone on for some time when her brother discovered it. You know how anything of that sort is regarded in Ireland? The girl's character, at any rate, was gone. Poor Dermot was at his wit's end, what with shame, and remorse, and his own affection for her, and the reproaches which he knew would be heaped upon him from all sides, and the end of it was that he took her off to

Cork one morning, and married her before a registrar."

"And his father found it out?"

"Why, of *course*. Such a thing couldn't but be found out sooner or later. At first he was simply indignant. But when Dermot told him that he was *married* to her—to a girl, remember, who had run about the place barefoot, weeded the walks, and picked the gooseberries—married to a Murrough, to one of the proudest people in all Ireland, and the vainest of their blood—there was a frightful scene. Both men had tremendous tempers once they were roused, though no one would have guessed it from seeing them on ordinary occasions. It ended by Lord Kilconnell ordering his son out of the house, and by Dermot retorting that he would never set foot in it again if his father went down on his knees to him to do so. He left that night with his wife, and took her abroad, though where they lived, or *how* they lived, no one knew, for he hadn't a farthing of his own. Lord Kilconnell's anger prevented him from writing for a long time, but at last the silence frightened him, and no doubt he was longing all the time to be friends again with Dermot, for he tried to discover the young couple's whereabouts. Whether he did so or not I don't know, but one morning, about three years ago, he received a letter telling him that Dermot was dead, he had died after a few days' illness of typhoid fever in some small town in France—Caen, I think."

"Poor man!   Poor man!" I ejaculated, looking across at the woods in all their autumn glory, and at a little sailing boat which was just rounding the next green point.   "How did he take it?" I added.

"He was found by one of the servants half-an-hour afterwards, lying with his head upon the hearth-rug below that big portrait of poor Dermot, which, in spite of his disgrace, always hung over the fireplace. He nearly died, and when he came to himself, and began to get about again, he was feeble and almost childish —seemed to have grown twenty years older in that one miserable fortnight. He is better now, but his memory is often astray, and he doesn't seem able to rouse himself to take an interest in anything."

"And the widow?"

"Money was sent to her, and she was told, I believe, that a certain yearly sum would be hers, but that she was to keep away from the place, or it would be immediately stopped. There was no boy, happily, but I am told that there was a little girl, though to the best of my belief Lord Kilconnell knows nothing about her. He stayed away for a year, but since then he has come down from time to time, generally without being expected, and this year he has spent nearly the whole summer here. He is one of the very few landlords in this part of the county who has never had any difficulties with his people. They pity him—and in Ireland, as you know, that goes a long way. 'The poor ould lard! God comfort him, the misfortunate crater!' a woman said to me not long since, and that seems to be the general sentiment. Now that Dermot is dead, all their old liking for him too has revived, and they feel kindly towards his father for his sake. Lord Kilconnell comes to see us now and then, and we try to get him to stay dinner, but he has grown very shy, though he used to be so sociable. Now that you are here I will ask him again. He will be glad, perhaps, to see you, and you can talk about old times."

"Do," said I, "I should like very much to see him again."

A few days later, Lord Kilconnell came across the Sound, in the course of the afternoon, and was induced, with some little difficulty, to stay for dinner. He was indeed greatly changed since I had seen him last. Then, though no longer young, he had been a striking-looking man ; noticeable amongst the youngest for his good looks, amongst the brightest for the quick flash and flow of his wit. Now he was bent, old, enfeebled, one might say extinguished. His faculties did not seem to be any of them actually gone, but the first blur of age had passed over them. You might have compared him to a singer who had lost her high notes. His memory had not exactly failed, but the power of perspective was no longer there. The quickness of his perceptions had gone, and his mind moved slowly, and chiefly in old and long-familiar ruts.

My friends were excessively hospitable, and it was rarely that we sat down to dinner without two or three unexpected guests appearing. Most of these self-elected guests were yacht-owners, or members of the Yacht Club at Queenstown, so that a great deal of yachting talk went on, much of which was so excessively technical as to be over my head, and practically unintelligible. On this occasion there happened to be only one other guest besides Lord Kil-connell, a rather deaf old gentleman known as Commander Coote ; an unmitigated bore, but a local institution, and as such tolerated, if not relished.   Commander Coote's one thought day and night was of yachts and yachting, indeed I never heard him open his lips upon any other subject.   Lord Kilconnell, having been a noted yacht-owner in his day, he on this occasion directed his conversation chiefly to him; pertinaciously recalling former seafaring experiences, which he fished up from the oozy depths of his memory, despite the evident disrelish of the other man for the subject.

"Dodger, now!" he began again, when we had hoped that the topic was momentarily shelved.   "You remember, Dodger, my Lord, he who owned the *Shrimp?*   When you knew him she was a yawl, wasn't she? well, before that he had a cutter, and after that a schooner; but they were all *Shrimps.*   Poor old Dodger, and he has gone to the shrimps himself now!" he added cheerfully.   "Died somewhere near the Azores, and was buried at sea.   Always said he meant to be buried at sea, and so he was.   Queer chap, Dodger!"

There was a pause, but our old Man of the Sea had not done with his reminiscences.   "Sir Wheeler Jones.   You knew Sir Wheeler when he was Commodore of the Yacht Squadron, didn't you, my Lord?" he presently began again. "He was another queer one; by the Lord, yes!

Do you remember the time he applied to the Admiralty for leave to flog his men? Oh, you may exclaim, ladies, but it is quite true. Ask his Lordship if it isn't. Of course they wouldn't hear of anything of the kind, and only laughed at him. But what do you think he did? Hired a fresh crew, and gave them fivepence-ha'penny a day extra on the understanding that he was to be allowed to flog them if he chose! And they agreed to it, too, fast enough, only one ill-conditioned cur of a fellow, whom he had given a dozen to for something, had him up before a Plymouth jury, and got damages to the tune of five hundred pounds. Rum old codger, Jones! He's dead, too. Got rheumatic fever that time the *Cormorant* went down outside Falmouth Harbour, and never stood straight again. I remember his coming on board the *Cuttlefish* at Cowes with two sticks under his arms, and his face twisted all awry! Dalby is another that's gone, he dropped at Constantinople of the dropsy. Gad, I believe you and I are about the last of the old lot, my Lord, and I suppose we shall be slipping our anchor pretty soon, too, eh? Ha! ha!"

Lord Kilconnell bowed sadly, and replied that it was probable. His manner was very dreamy, though as full of old-world courtesy

and dignity as ever.   After dinner he came and
sat beside me, a little apart from the rest of the
circle.   We talked about old times, for though
I had never known him very well, we had met
from time to time, and I knew a good many of
his relations.   Now and then a momentary
lapse of consciousness seemed to come over him
—a sort of film over the mind—his eyes would
grow misty, and an oddly fixed expression would
come into his face.   Then the attack, whatever
it was, would pass off, and he would resume
his courtly deferential talk as if nothing had
happened.

I think he enjoyed his evening, in spite of
old Coote's reminiscences, for after that he came
pretty often.   It was lovely weather, and he
would land of an afternoon from his boat, and
walk up the gravel path which led from the
little pier, two of his dogs generally following
at his heels.   Here he would find us sitting
about upon the lawn;   the younger people
playing tennis;   we of an older and staider
generation chatting, or sipping our tea to an
accompaniment of lapping waves;   the reflections
from the little fiord performing fantastic dances
upon the grass and tree-trunks.   Now and then
a fishing or pleasure boat would appear, looking
like some oddly-shaped white blossom amongst

the leaves of the trees ; the soft, poetic sunlight
of the South of Ireland streaming the while in
uneven bands over the sward, and bringing out
fresh eccentricities of tint amongst the orange
and liver-coloured begonias which were at that
time my hostess's especial pride and joy.

We took as little notice of his arrival
as we could, that being evidently what suited
him best. He would settle himself into one
of the basket-chairs, and either talk, or sit
silently stroking the silken head of Sheelah,
his favourite red setter, who never seemed
easy unless she was cuddling her nose into
her master's hand. Sometimes he would grow
quite brilliant for a few minutes ; all his
old animation reviving. It was rarely, however, that the flash lasted more than a few
minutes. The impulse would die out, as
if extinguished, and he would drop into
silence, and sit there, dreamily twisting Sheelah's silky ears through his fingers. His love
of pet animals included children, and there
was one little girl of the house who shared
with Sheelah the right of standing beside his
knee, and having her head stroked. One day
he arrived with a small black bundle stowed
away under his elbow, and inquired for her.
" Where's Dodo ? where's my little Dodo ? "

Dodo was not long in appearing, and received a small black retriever puppy, with the wettest of noses, and tightest of curled fleeces, exactly like a toy lamb's. It was a piece of unusual munificence, I was told ; the one point upon which Lord Kilconnell had always been accounted churlish by his neighbours being his dogs. He had the best breed of setters and retrievers in the whole South of Ireland, and had hardly ever been known to give one of them away.

I stayed on that autumn in Queenstown Bay longer than I had originally intended ; another visit which I had proposed paying having had to be given up. I was not in the least loath. The place was delightful ; the people kindness itself. We made daily expeditions in my host's steam launch. We assisted at the departure of sundry " White Stars " and " Cunarders " on their Atlantic voyages. We dawdled about the garden, and discussed horticulture, upon which subject my entertainers were both of them finished experts. I fell into the habit, too, of going over nearly daily to Castle Murrough. Not that it is a castle, by the way, any more than this implement I am writing with is a stiletto, but that in Ireland is a well-understood figure of speech.

Lord Kilconnell was always alone, and always received me kindly, as though rather pleased at the encroachment upon his solitude. There was something to me very touching in his relations with his immediate retainers, most of whom had been born, and were growing grey, in his service. He was often extremely fractious; swearing at them upon small occasions with old-fashioned vigour, forgetful apparently for the moment of my presence. Upon these occasions the culprit would stand, hat in hand, listening to the storm of words with an air of deprecation. Almost always, however, there was a look of forbearance lurking somewhere in the corner of his eye, which seemed to neutralize, and, as it were, reverse the relative positions. Of this look Lord Kilconnell himself would sometimes seem conscious, for with a final " pish !" he would break off, and hurry away at a rate which obliged me to scuttle along in somewhat undignified fashion in order to catch him up.

After three weeks of this ideal weather, a change occurred. For some hours an ominous calm "raged," as an eloquent Cork newspaper once expressed it. Then the wind got up; the rain fell; and a storm descended. Never had I seen so vindictive a storm ! The flowers in the garden were broken off and scattered like chaff over the walks; the trees rocked; branches were broken from them with a sudden snap; everything seemed to be seized, throttled, destroyed; the whole grace and beauty of the season wrested from it at one fell swoop. In all directions the leaves were being flung about like flights of frightened birds; the birds themselves tossed like things devoid of volition about the sky. There was something cruel in this convulsive struggle of all Nature against the invisible onslaught. The friendly trees; the brightly-tinted creepers; the orderly walks and pretty flower-borders, all wore that peculiar look of pathos which clings to mild and orderly natures when brought into contact with a power before which they are helpless to do anything but to suffer. We gathered at the windows, and could do nothing but look on at this scene of ruin, unable to interpose a finger.

Next morning, when the storm had somewhat abated, I took an umbrella and mackintosh, and crossed over the little channel to Castle Murrough, where I found Lord Kilconnell, alone upon the terrace, with Sheelah at his heels. He proposed that we should go for a turn, and I readily agreed. Here too everything looked battered. The clouds hung grey and swollen over the headlands. The woods dripped at every pore. I should have preferred a drier walk, but Lord Kilconnell turned off the terrace along a path that took us through a low-lying part of the woods towards the shore. It was a dank one at any time, and felt doubly so that day. A heavy scent of decaying vegetation met us as we advanced. One or two forlorn little summer-houses rose rather absurdly here and there, and at one point stood an aviary, in which a sulky-looking eagle was hopping disconsolately, who fluttered, and shrieked a discordant shriek of anger at the sight of Sheelah.

We crossed one or two level bridges of logs, below which a thick current of water, swollen with the rain, was slipping into a little lake, and presently came to a point where the path branched ; one part leading to the sea-shore, the other to a small enclosed flower-garden, lying under a rocky bank.

A little girl was standing close to the gate of this garden with a bunch of flowers in her hands ; not garden flowers, but common loose-strifes and such-like, which she must have gathered along the edge of the stream. She was a pretty little creature, with light hair, and beautiful dark-blue eyes, and was dressed poorly, yet not quite like a peasant's child, in a short black frock, with a band round her waist, well-fitting stockings and shoes, and a straw-hat with a shabby black ribbon. Lord Kilconnell, with his usual liking for children, stopped to lay a couple of fingers upon her head, and ask her her name, to which she made a blushing and inarticulate reply, and we passed on into the garden. Sheelah remained a moment after us to sniff solemnly round the child; which done, as if satisfied with the result, she also trotted leisurely after her master.

The garden, which was larger than it appeared to be from the outside, ended in an oval curve, overhung with a high cliff or bank of rocks and earth. A sound of digging reached our ears, coming apparently from somewhere underground, and on looking closely I perceived the mouth of a passage or cave, which seemed to run underground for some distance, and from which the sound proceeded.

Lord Kilconnell started, and half turned as if to leave the place. At the same moment the sound ceased, and a man appeared at the entrance of the cave; a big stalwart fellow, broad-shouldered and grey-eyed. Perceiving

his master, he also started, and lifted his cap
with an air of embarrassment. Whereupon
Lord Kilconnell apparently relinquished the
idea of retreating, and returned the man's bow
with a friendly nod.

" Good-day, Phelim.   Did Mr. Connor desire
you to clear out that passage ? " he asked.

" 'Deed no, me Lard ; 'twas meself thought
maybe 'twould be better. 'Tis three years, yer
Lardship knows, since 'twas——"

Lord Kilconnell put up his hand hastily.

" Yes, yes, I know.   All right, only don't
do more than is absolutely necessary. This is
a nice plant of araucaria, is it not ? " he continued to me, pointing to a shrub of sickly
aspect, half suffocated by grasses and wild briar.

I replied that it was, which was perfectly
untrue, and we continued looking at it for some
minutes in silence.

While we were still standing in the same
place I chanced to glance towards the entrance
of the cave, and perceived to my astonishment
that the man to whom Lord Kilconnell had just
spoken was going through the most extraordinary
series of pantomimes. With his head turned
in our direction, he was flinging his hands, now
upwards, now forwards, with a gesture directed
towards some one at the other end of the

garden, evidently with the desire of preventing
that person's approach.   Curious to see to whom
this pantomime was addressed, I turned, and saw
that the little girl whom we had already noticed
had followed us into the garden, and was now
standing a little way off, her small face puckered
into a not unnatural expression of bewilderment.
A moment later Lord Kilconnell too turned, and
a smile lit up his eyes.

"Well, little girl.   Come to look at the
garden, have you?" said he.   "There, there,
don't be frightened.   Go and pick some flowers
for yourself.   Who is she, Phelim?" he added,
turning to the man, and speaking in a lower
tone.

But Phelim's face had assumed that expression of impenetrable stolidity which every
one who knows Ireland is intimately acquainted
with.

"Who's what, me Lard?" he inquired, in a
tone of admirably natural astonishment.

Lord Kilconnell stepped a little aside, and
pointed to the child.

Phelim scratched his head with an air of blank
unrecognition.

"I dunno, me Lard.   Maybe 'tis one of
thim lodger's childer that do be comin' for
the say water.   Bad scran to them for lettin'

her trispass over your Lardship's grounds. Will I send her away before she does be spoilin' the plants?"

"You never saw her before?"

"Is it me, me Lard? Sure, how would I? 'Tis here to-day, and gone to-morrow, that sort is."

"Very well, as you know nothing about her, I'll take her back myself, and find out who she belongs to. Come here, little girl, take this lady's hand, and come along with us."

Attracted apparently by his voice, the child had gradually approached of her own accord along the walk. Lord Kilconnell advanced a few steps to meet her, and they stood facing one another. Then I saw an odd, startled expression come into his face, and he put his hand quickly before his eyes, as if seized with giddiness. The little girl seemed also suddenly to be overtaken with fright, for, darting past us like a rabbit, she rushed up to Phelim Delaney, and, seizing him by the knees, pressed her little head tightly against his body as if for protection.

Sheelah barked with sudden excitement. Lord Kilconnell wheeled round like a hawk.

"Why the child knows you perfectly well, Phelim! What the devil did you mean, you impudent rascal, by telling me you had never seen her before?" he exclaimed angrily.

"Thin indade I humbly ask yer Lardship's pardon—whist, darlin' child, don't cry. Sure, I didn't want to be bringin' them into trubble, an' that's just the gospel truth. Dacint people the Slatterlys are; ould tinents of your Lardship's and your Lardship's father before it; safe to the day with their rint, as your Lardship knows."

"Oh, the child is a Slatterly, is she?"

"She is, yer Lardship, that's just what she is, Aleesha Mary Slatterly is her name. She'd tell ye so herself, only it's dashed she is just now, not being used to the quality."

"Every Slatterly I've ever seen was *dark*," Lord Kilconnell said, looking at the child's hair with an expression of suspicion.

"And that's true, for your Lardship. This one now, she has a little shister at home—born the same minute as herself—Rosabel Anna is her name—whose hair is as black as the tail of a crow. One ov thim has taken all the light colour, an' the other all the dark, I'm thinkin'," Phelim ended, with an inimitable air of mature reflection upon the subject.

In spite of this last piece of circumstantial evidence, Lord Kilconnell seemed unconvinced.

His eyes rested with an expression of trouble, of growing perplexity, upon the child's fair head.

"Come here, little girl," he said at last gently. "Let her go, Phelim, damn you!" he added with sudden fierceness, seeing that the man and child were remarkably unwilling to part company.

"She's dashed, the cratur," the former said apologetically. "She's afraid of being skelped by her mither for troubbling your Lardship and the leddy,"—with a sudden piteous glance in my direction, which seemed to intimate a desire to establish some channel of communication with me.

"She has got a mother, has she?" Lord Kilconnell asked quickly.

"A mither is it? Niver a mither in the warld, bad cess to me tongue for lyin'. Sure her mither died the day she was born, an' that's why she has the black on her, the cratur!"

This being scarcely a sufficient reason for a little girl of five or six years old wearing mourning, I here indulged in a slight laugh, on hearing which Phelim gazed at me with an expression of piteous resentment which ought to have melted a stone.

Lord Kilconnell was not apparently inclined

to give up his point. "Come here, little girl,"
he said again. Then when the child had re-
luctantly approached a few steps—"Tell me
your name, pretty one, and don't be afraid.
Nobody is going to hurt you," he said, stooping
down so as to bring his face more on a level with
her tiny one.

The child looked up at him with eyes full
of frightened tears—beautiful eyes they were,
and as blue as a blue nemophila. Then,
when he had repeated his question, "Uncle
Phelim thaid"—she whimpered; then suddenly stopped short, putting up both hands
to her eyes, and screwing them vigorously into
the corners.

Lord Kilconnell started upright, and looked
at the man over the child's head. It was a
look full of anger; of passionate resentment,
and of something else that was almost, I
thought, like fear.

"'Tis a way they have of callin' me uncle,"
that inveterate perverter of facts responded
shamelessly. "'Tis along ov an ould song—
'Teddy the tailor's uncle,' I do be singin' thim,"
he added, although his lip trembled as he spoke,
and his cheek, I saw, had visibly paled.

This was too much for Lord Kilconnell's
patience. "Don't stand there lying to me, you

H

scoundrel!" he thundered. "Tell me this instant who the child is, or by God I'll——" His hands, which he had clenched, suddenly opened, and he caught at the air as if trying to find something to support him.

Alarmed, I seized hold of him, Phelim ran to the other side, and between us we kept him upon his feet. I felt sure that he was going to have a stroke, but by a great effort of will he recovered, and looked round; first at the child, who had shrunk away behind us, and then at the man, who stood trembling, and scarcely less frightened beside him.

"You needn't tell me any more lies," he said slowly and feebly; "I know whose child she is. I know——"

Suddenly he stood upright, shaking off our hold as he did so, and, seizing the child's hand, he started away at a rapid walk.

I followed, alarmed, and not in the least knowing what he proposed doing. We left the garden, Sheelah trotting after us, and turned in the direction of the sea. I heard other steps, not Sheelah's, behind us, and knew, without turning round, that Phelim had also followed, unable doubtless to endure the suspense of remaining behind. Luckily we had not far to go. Before long we came to a good-sized cabin, standing in the middle of a wood, and almost hidden by a dense growth of over-grown laurels and tall dilapidated elder-trees, whose blossoms were filling the air with their heavy narcotic scent. The door of the cabin was shut, and the whole house appeared to be deserted. Lord Kilconnell however went straight up to it, and struck a single resounding knock upon the door with his walking-stick.

There was a minute's pause—a pause apparently of consternation. Then it was cautiously opened, and an old woman in a blue homespun dress and striped shawl peered cautiously out. At sight of the two who stood there she uttered a scream of terror, and ran hastily back, evidently with the intention of giving a signal to some one within. She had no time to do so. Quicker than thought Lord Kilconnell followed, I after him, Sheelah after me, and we all stood inside the cabin. There in the middle of the floor stood a young woman, dressed in black, who had evidently just sprung to her feet, for she still held a little stocking that she was knitting in her hand. A handsome creature, with brown hair and grey eyes, like Phelim's.

There was a pause, full of, I knew not what, ominous suggestions. Then the girl — she

seemed to be little more—sank upon her knees,
and began to sob.   At first hardly audible, her
sobs gradually rose in the silence, louder and
louder until the whole cabin seemed to echo
with them.   The old woman caught the infec-
tion, and stood rocking herself to and fro, wailing as if in the presence of a corpse.   It gave
me the strangest, the most overwhelming sense
of death ; an uncanny, eerie sensation, such as I
had never felt before.   It seemed to affect Lord
Kilconnell in much the same way.   The impulse, whatever it was, that had brought him
to the cabin seemed to desert him.   His anger
appeared to die suddenly away.   He glanced
vaguely at me, as if to ask what he was to do in
this unforeseen dilemma.   A fresh impulse, and
this time the determining one, came from the
little girl, whose hand he still retained.   Pulling
it away, she ran forward, and flung herself upon
her mother, with a loud cry of distress, and
from this refuge looked back pitifully at the
old man, her blue eyes flooded with tears.   Then
I knew why her eyes had seemed to me from
the first familiar.   They were those of Dermot
Murrough, come to life again in the face of a
little child.

It was the turning-point !   Lord Kilconnell's
courage, his endurance, so long maintained,

broke down.   Covering his face with his hands, he fell into helpless sobbing—the heavy, slow-coming tears of an old man.   They were the first tears, I imagine, that he had shed since Dermot Murrough died.

My story is finished.   Mrs. Dermot Murrough left her mother's cabin the next day, but she was *not* turned adrift.   There happened to be a good-sized cottage vacant, with a garden, but no other land attached to it, and into this she and her child were formally inducted.   Lord and Lady Saggart were furious, I was told, and wanted, right or wrong, to have the " shameless creature " driven from the property.   This, however, served her well rather than ill, there being few things Lord Kilconnell resented more than any hint of interference on the part of his little-loved eldest son.   Two or three evenings later I happened to be returning alone in the steam-launch, the rest of the party having got out to walk home.   The boatmen took me close under the Castle Murrough woods, and I lay back, and looked up at their tangled luxuriance, rising curve above curve—very brown and battered those curves had grown to look during the last fortnight.   The chimneys of the " Great House " were sending   out thin columns of smoke ; a squadron of rooks were swooping with much croaking clamour to their roost in the big elms ; the sunset light was palpitating in rapidly paling dots and streaks upon the leaves ; upon the tops of the dilapidated gazebos and aviaries, and upon the little boats curtsying at their anchorage in the clear brown water. And higher up, upon the broad gravel terrace which lay immediately in front of the house, I could see three figures—those of an old man, a dog, and a little girl—who were pacing leisurely to and fro in the gathering dusk.

OF THE INFLUENCE OF ASSASSIN-
ATION UPON A LANDSCAPE

THERE are places in Ireland—in many other parts of the world no doubt also, but one can only speak of what one knows best—at sight of which one says to oneself instinctively, "Something *must* have happened here ! There must be some story about *this* place !" In nine cases out of ten such impressions are the purest moonshine. Your highly suggestive-looking spot has no history, or none that any one has ever heard of, and it is some thoroughly matter-of-fact-looking place, or some place over which an air of delusive calm seems to brood, where the real tragedies or the real horrors have occurred.

I remember a picnic once upon a time that was dreadfully marred by a forgetfulness of this fact. It was quite an impromptu picnic, and had been suddenly arranged by my hostess and myself, who had offered to go on ahead, and to

get it ready before the rest of the party came up.
To save ourselves trouble, as well as utilize a
pony-carriage which carried our provisions, we
had selected a spot close to the high-road, but
then I must explain that this was in Donegal,
and in Donegal high-roads are often exceedingly
exclusive places, and this particular spot we had
hit upon appeared to be all that the least sociable
of picnic-makers could desire.   A fern-covered
bank at the back, cutting off any chance of cold
wind ; a level space in front upon which even
wine-glasses might stand unsupported ; a salmon
stream tumbling and twinkling in bubbling
yellow curves a little to the left ; a long row
of melancholy stern-faced mountains.   Add to
these a really magnificent chicken pasty to serve
as crown and centre to the whole picture, and
what more could the heart, the stomach, or the
imagination desire ?   We looked about us—at
the mountains, at the salmon-stream, and at the
chicken pasty—and said to one another that
our selection could not possibly have been
improved upon.

Alas for our pride !   Hardly had we completed our preparations, before, far down the
road, the tall figure of my host, who was also
my friend's husband, was seen advancing rapidly
towards us.   Even while still a long way off there

were evident signs of disturbance about his aspect;
his very coat tails seemed to swing and sway with
indignation. What was it? we asked ourselves
with some apprehension. Could any disaster
have happened in the short space of time that
had elapsed since we parted? That our own
praiseworthy doings could by any possibility be
the subject of these demonstrations seemed at
first too preposterous to be believed. And yet—
No! Yes! yes, it really *was!* it really did seem
to be at *us* that he was pointing, at *us* that he
was waving his arms so vehemently and indignantly.

We were not long left in any doubt upon
that subject.

"Take away those things! Good heavens,
what could have induced you to stick them
in *that* place? Put them away at once, before
any one sees them," he cried in imperative accents
to his wife, and, without deigning to explain
matters further, sped off indignantly down the
road.

Now there are occasions—few, I admit, but
still some—when a guest has a right to fly
into a rage with her host, and this I felt to be
one of them. " Why should we not set out our
picnic where we chose? If we were good enough
and kind enough to take the trouble of arranging

it for other people, what business was it of theirs to interfere with our selection?" I looked in speechless indignation at my companion, and was pleased to see that even her usual equanimity seemed to be disturbed; so at least I judged by the air of firm wifely authority with which, after a moment's delay, and a businesslike nod to me, she followed the coat tails down the road.

She came back after a minute's colloquy, looking rather paler than before, but evidently satisfied.

"John was perfectly right," she said, indicating the still agitated coat tails. "Do you know what that place is?"—pointing to our poor feast which still sadly encumbered the ground. "It is the very spot where that unhappy man Nolan was murdered last March year! He was shot, you may remember, on his way back from the assizes where he had gone to give evidence. John had to be present at the inquest—so naturally knew it again directly he saw it."

There was nothing further to be said, and as I helped to bundle away our unhappy arrangements, I was obliged to admit the justice of "John's" suddenly awakened wrath, with the private reservation, however, that, if eminently satisfactory so far as he was concerned, it could hardly be called an addition to the pleasantness of Donegal picnics.

This only too truthful little anecdote is, however, merely incidental, and has no other connection with the following tale than as an illustration of the always appropriate truism that it is unsafe to go entirely by appearances. It is not in places of this kind, moreover, that impressions such as those I have alluded to ever grow fixed and stereotyped. Nature—heaven bless her for it !—is the most discreet, the most delicate of housekeepers, and knows how to make smooth her ruffled shrines, and to re-adorn her desecrated sanctuaries, with a deftness and a rapidity which soon turns even the worst of our poor human Golgothas into green Edens, and freshly blooming Arcadias. It is in places where she does not get fair play, or in places where we have overlaid her handiwork with our own clumsier fabrics, that the sense of gloom and of tragedy seems to get incorporated as it were in the very stones. Setting aside houses, which of course carry their histories, sometimes their very destinies, written upon their faces, there are smaller pieces of man's handiwork which possess this rather questionable prerogative. Entrance-gates, for instance, are often very significant objects, and nowhere more significant or more characteristic than in Ireland.

Who that knows that country at all familiarly has not made acquaintance with some ferociously frowning gateway, all crenellations and castellated copings ; a gateway beset with rows of apparently impregnable battlements, or flanked by towers pierced with sinister slits—evidently for the convenience of archers. A gateway whose mingled ferocity and exclusiveness would strike consternation into our very souls did we not know—as, if we belong to the neighbourhood, we naturally do know,—that a few yards to the right or left of it we shall come upon some friendly ragged hedge, through the gaps in which the cows are in the habit of sauntering out at their pleasure, in order to enjoy an illicit mouthful of grass upon the Queen's high-road.

Again there are other gateways, which if less threatening than these, seem to have attuned themselves to the melancholy elements of our natures, and to be laying themselves out—sometimes to an even theatrical degree—to working upon those elements. Broken, bulging, discoloured, falling in pieces ; a prey to gods and men ; ill-used by weather, by passing boys, by passing cows, they seem to say, " We were not *always* thus ! We too have known happier

days ! We have been opened by eager hands !
We have clanged cheerfully after departing
guests ! We were reared in much hope ! We
have shut in much hospitality. We have been
the portals to much friendliness ! Look on us !
Pity us ! ye that pass by ! "

Towards such almost professional applicants
for public pity, it may be well for prudent
people to preserve a somewhat cautious attitude, and not allow themselves to be drawn
out into sympathy without a due inquiry into
the circumstances of each individual case.
There are other gateways, however, which
do not appeal in so histrionic a fashion to
the merest tripper, but which, to those who
are behind the scenes, are known to have been
really the portals to a good deal of genuine
tragedy ; sometimes to an amount of sheer suffering, which it would seem to need a Dante or
an Æschylus to do justice to.

The particular gateway which I have at this
moment in my mind is not distinguished over
other deserted gateways in any marked or
demonstrative manner. It is dilapidated-look-
ing, certainly, and the avenue to which it
leads is greener than many grass fields ; green
with that peculiarly clinging vegetation which
grows upon disused roadways ; but beyond this

there is nothing that would oblige you, if you were passing by, to stop and look at it—*unless* you knew its history.

Mount Kennedy—as the house to which it leads is called — has for nearly a century been uninhabited, and at present belongs to a well-to-do land-owner in the neighbourhood. It has often been a matter of surprise, especially to strangers, why he should like to keep anything so forlorn close to his own rather noticeably spick-and-span abode. Probably the explanation is to be found in the fact that it had, even before his time, reached a stage of dilapidation which rendered any hope of letting, or otherwise disposing of it, hopeless, while, on the other hand, there is a well-understood reluctance in Ireland to pulling down and utterly abolishing the memory of those who have once "reigned" in any given spot; a reluctance naturally increased in this case by the peculiar circumstances under which Mount Kennedy passed out of the hands of its former owner.

A small but fascinating little stream, rapid, babbling, confidential, ending in a tossing imp of a waterfall, is only to be reached down this green approach, a circumstance which has several times brought me within sight of the derelict house. Last time I found myself there I was alone, and curiosity induced me to approach nearer to it than I had ever hitherto done. On doing so I discovered that part of one side of the porch had fallen in, doubtless from the rotting of some of the timbers beneath, so that, although the front door still remained bolted and barred, I could peep in, and make out nearly the whole of the entrance hall. It was a small square hall, and from one of its mouldering walls a couple of huge elks' horns still branched colossally. Beyond, through a half-open door, I could see a corner of what had evidently been one of the living-rooms, with part of an enormous fireplace, black, or rather greenish-grey, with that insidious mouldiness which, in this climate, sooner or later overtakes everything.

There was something piteous in the suggestion thus called up of what had doubtless once been a warm hearth, lit, as hearths in this neighbourhood are wont to be, by a mountain of glowing turf; now for ever blackened, and given over to gloom, emptiness, and the extreme of desolation. Where I stood the air was warm and comforting; the trees around were soft with greenish yellows or dusky reds; an old disused graveyard which lay a little below the house proffered its appropriate quota of reflection, and I lingered a while, supping, half luxuriously, as one sometimes does, upon that sense of all-pervading melancholy which, when it does not come home too pressingly to oneself, is rarely without charm.

That something keener and sharper than such mild meditations would have been more appropriate to this particular scene I was already aware, though hardly to the extent which I realized after an opportunity, which I shortly afterwards enjoyed, of talking over the whole story with the son of an actual partaker in it. I will take up the thread of that story at what may be called its most dramatic moment, thus sparing you those preliminary *hums* and *haws* which are apt to be the bore of such recitals.

WHAT THE BAG CONTAINED

A poor plain man, sent to the shades below;
A poor kind man, whose kindness wrought his woe.
Who loved his home, his people, and his land,
Loved e'en his King—love hard to understand!
Good people, ye who live in easier days,
List to this tale.   Give it nor blame nor praise,
Only its simple moral lay to heart—
No peace had they who took the middle part.

LORD BALLYBROPHY was dreadfully disturbed. He was standing in his own deer-
park, looking down a long bracken glade, upon
one side of which lay a small triangular-shaped
wood, across which the sun was just then
shaking its last rays. He had dined, for it
was already seven o'clock, and four was the
fashionable dinner-hour a century ago in
Ireland. He had dined largely, liberally,
and had strolled forth to enjoy an hour's
saunter over the grass, previous to settling

down for the night to cards. All this was quite as it ought to be, yet his mind was most unaccustomarily disturbed, and what the cause of that disturbance was you are about to be informed.

It was a year when a good many Irish people's minds were disturbed—the still unforgotten year of 'Ninety-eight. For months the whole country had been ringing, first with alarms, then with the actual details of Rebellion. It was not that any pains had been spared by the executive of the day to hinder the misguided island from rushing upon its destruction. For nearly a year past an indefatigable soldiery had been allowed full discretion, and in their zeal for the cause of loyalty had spared no means to coerce recusants into the paths of order. The Commander-in-Chief who immediately preceded Lord Cornwallis was a man known to entertain the largest and most liberal ideas in this respect, and as such to be fully worthy of the confidence reposed in him by his superiors in England. At the time of which this story treats, the first scenes of the rising were already over, but the fire still in places burned fiercely, and that same system of energetic, and not always fantastically discriminating, discipline was still held to be indispensable.

This larger view of the matter was not, however, what was chiefly disturbing Lord Ballybrophy's mind. It was a smaller and a much more personal one. In his youth and early manhood his most intimate friend had been Eustace Kennedy, the son and heir of the owner of the neighbouring property of Mount Kennedy, the entrance gate of which stood nearly opposite to the Ballybrophy one. The two young men had been at College together; had stood by one another in not a few duels, and had seen together the bottom of more bowls of punch than it would be possible at this hour to enumerate. When, therefore, upon his father's death, Lord Ballybrophy had succeeded to the family estates, it had been an additional satisfaction in the lot to which a kind Providence had called him that his friend Eustace, whose father was also dead, would be his nearest neighbour, and would be able to help him in carrying out not a few local reforms upon which his own energetic mind was already actively engaged.

Alas for these anticipations! "Constancy lives in realms above, and life is thorny, and

youth is vain," and before many years the two
men had quarrelled bitterly, and the cause of
this quarrel had been no other than that
ridiculous little piece of triangular woodland,
at which Lord Ballybrophy was at this moment
gazing !

To begin with, it was a " Naboth's vineyard,"
a fragment of the smaller property which had
got enclosed, as happens sometimes, in the larger
one. Lord Ballybrophy would willingly have
purchased it at many times its value. Eustace
Kennedy, who was always more or less in want
of money, would probably as willingly have
sold it. Unfortunately it was impossible. A
strict entail barred him from doing so, added
to which, at the farther end of the wood lay
a graveyard, still used by the Kennedy family,
and as such inalienable.

It was not the mere fact of the existence of
this Naboth's vineyard so much as certain circumstances which arose out of its ownership
which had caused the breach. Lord Ballybrophy was, even in his youth, a strict dis-
ciplinarian ; one of those men to whom the
belief in a natural hierarchy is almost a matter
of religion. Believing as he did in the inherent
difference between—let us' say pewter and silver
—he held it to be the duty of the latter in

all things to direct, to control, and if necessary to coerce the former. Now upon these points Eustace Kennedy was deplorably lax. He was emphatically what people call "easygoing." Probably he had always been so, but it was only when he became a neighbouring proprietor that the trait revealed itself to Lord Ballybrophy in all its heinousness. He did not, for instance, care about game-preserving himself, and what was much worse, he did not sufficiently concern himself about the game rights of others. He allowed the Mount Kennedy property to drift along in a comfortable, happy-go-lucky, time-immemorial fashion. His tenants did as they liked. Their rents were never raised. Their wives might rear as many chickens and pigs as they chose. Their children were allowed to pick sticks through all the Kennedy woods. And if a stout gossoon knocked over a hare or a rabbit, and carried it home under his rags to his mother's pot, Eustace Kennedy was capable of winking hard, and declining to prosecute the offender, even when the deed was brought home to him in the clearest and most unmistakable light.

All this was very painful to his friend, the rather that, owing to the position of that un-

lucky little Naboth's vineyard, the Kennedy
"tinints," their wives, children, chickens, pigs,
and families generally, were continually trespassing upon the Ballybrophy property. No
matter what leg-breaking man-traps, no matter
what hand- or foot-destroying fences were
put up, under, or over, such fences those
"tinints" would manage to crawl, or otherwise
get. Walking in his woods, Lord Ballybrophy
would continually come upon traces of recent
depredations. The marks of bare feet upon
the poached mud of a gap would stare him in
the face. Broken twigs from his young planta-
tions would litter the ground. Worse still, there
were dark suspicions in the form of rabbits or
hares believed to have been trapped, and always,
as his gamekeepers were ready to take oath, by
"thim owdacious divils" from the other side
of the fence !

At last the fire, long smouldering, burst into
open flame. A boy was caught red-handed
with a rabbit in his possession, which he was
taking home to his grandmother. He was not
actually captured upon the Ballybrophy estate,
but upon the limit of that wood which broke
like a splinter through the centre of it, and so
grievously marred its symmetry. This being
the case, it was clear that the rabbit in question

must be a Ballybrophy rabbit, and as such Lord Ballybrophy was entirely within his rights in insisting that his friend Eustace Kennedy should prosecute the offender.

This Eustace Kennedy peremptorily declined to do. As it happened, the boy was the grand-son of an old pensioner and former servant of the Kennedys, a certain Thaddeus or Thady O'Roon, a privileged old being, united to his master by one of those odd ties, half-feudal, half-personal, of which our more advanced civil-ization has well-nigh forgotten the existence. With that disproportionate vehemence which was one of his failings, Eustace Kennedy swore, and moreover swore before witnesses, that rather than break old Thady's heart by sending his grandson to jail, possibly to the gallows—for the game laws were no joke in those days—every rabbit in the county of C—— might, for aught he cared, be killed and eaten.

Lord Ballybrophy's patience, long tried, fairly broke down under this unneighbourly conduct. Mr. Kennedy, he retorted with a formality which only characterized him in moments of displeasure, must choose between the O'Roon family and himself. If his regard for those interesting persons was of so excessively tender a nature that he preferred it to his duties as a landlord, and to the ordinary courtesies of a neighbour and a gentleman, Lord Ballybrophy regretted the circumstance, but could not, in duty to himself, continue to hold further friendly relations with one whose views of the becoming stood in such diametrical contrast to his own.

The quarrel, thus handsomely inaugurated, grew and deepened as it is the fashion of quarrels to do. Eustace Kennedy made one or two efforts towards a reconciliation, but since nothing would induce him to yield in the main point, his efforts made matters rather worse than better. The close propinquity of the once friends, now foes, added fuel to the fire. Perceiving how matters stood, the underlings on both sides made haste to pour oil upon the flames. In short, it was as pretty a quarrel as the county of C—— had enjoyed for many a year past.

So matters had gone on nearly up to the time at which this little history is laid. In the interval both gentlemen had married, but neither of those events had produced the slightest relaxation in their mutual attitude. The ladies, consequently, were all but strangers to one another, and no intercourse had been kept up between the two houses, although so near were they that the graveyard belonging to the

Kennedy family actually constituted an inconveniently conspicuous object from the windows of the "Great House," as Lord Ballybrophy's residence was called in the neighbourhood.

If private affairs were stationary, public ones meanwhile had been moving rapidly, and the unhappy country had been drifting nearer and nearer to that vortex of rebellion into which a large portion of it was destined to plunge. Then it was that that laxity of principles so long obvious to his neighbour and quondam friend began to be generally observed in Eustace Kennedy. It was not that he shared in the revolutionary sentiments with which many of his countrymen were at that time saturated ; far less that he took any personal part in the rising. It was that as a magistrate and a local magnate he was again deplorably "lax," and it was this laxity which proved his ruin. Even the fierce heat of a religious and social panic could not turn the too mild milk of his nature to anything resembling gall. He even, contrary to his customary indolence, went the length of remonstrating with the local military authorities against what seemed to him their excess of zeal, especially as to their mode of extracting evidence, which he actually went so far as to assert was contrary to the dictates of common humanity.

That these observations produced no result, beyond causing him to be regarded as a firebrand and a favourer of rebels, goes without saying ; human nature being so constituted that only one violent sentiment can, as a rule, be comfortably entertained by us at any given time.

Nor had Mr. Kennedy the prudence, when he discovered the impression produced, to change his tactics, and at once distinguish himself by a greater degree of zeal than his neighbours. On the contrary, when every other gentleman in the county either fled from home, or implored to have troops sent into his house for protection, he did neither; declaring that he felt no fears upon his own account, and repeating those uncomplimentary remarks with regard to the troops in question which had already produced so strong and so natural a feeling of resentment against himself.

Had he stated publicly that his Majesty King George III. had no right to the throne upon which he then sat, it would have been a less hazardous proceeding at the moment ! Not only every soldier in the district, but every official in Ireland was in arms against him. He became a marked man, and it was openly declared in official circles that Mr. Kennedy, of

Mount Kennedy, either was already a rebel, or would shortly be proved to be one.

Nor had the prophets long to wait. The Rebellion broke out; its leaders having been arrested in time, the command fell into any hands willing to take it up. A thousand wild schemes were proposed, and a certain number were attempted to be acted upon. There were hasty marches, or rather headlong scampers of frieze-coated levies, hither and thither about the county of C——. There were sundry isolated acts of hideous barbarity, combined with not a few acts of oddly unexpected kindliness and pitifulness. There were wild scenes of child-ish panic; and there were other scenes that for dare-devil courage and tenacity have not often been equalled by forces equally ill-armed and undisciplined. In the course of these various manœuvres it came into the heads of a certain portion of the rebel force to take posses-sion of the grounds of Mount Kennedy, and to establish a temporary camp upon the lawn. The owner's leave was not asked, so that his partici-pation in the arrangement was a purely negative one. Next morning the unwelcome visitors departed; smashing fences and outhouses, break-ing down gates, and generally destroying every-thing on which they could lay their hands, but giving—so it was subsequently sworn at his trial—three cheers for their unwilling entertainer as they went.

Those three cheers proved to be Eustace Kennedy's death-warrant !   On the ragged host poured ; shouting, gesticulating, yelling.   The attack that day was intended, I believe, to be a surprise ! The result was what might have been expected.   The suburbs of the nearest town were taken with yells of enthusiasm ; a little further on the rebels were met by a steady fire of musketry, before which their undisciplined force collapsed like a pricked balloon.   The slaughter was considerable.   Many of the unfortunate rebels tried to take refuge in the houses ; but the houses were set on fire by the soldiery, and . . . in short we are not called upon by the necessities of our tale to go further in this direction, and the reader will probably be thankful.   Punishment by the sword being over, judicial punishment followed.   A former sergeant, believed to have taken part with the rebels, was the first arrest made, the second was Mr. Eustace Kennedy of Mount Kennedy, who was triumphantly captured the next afternoon in his dining-room, while sitting at dinner there with his family.

The news of this successful arrest was brought

to Ballybrophy House the following morning by the officers quartered there, two of whom, a captain and a cornet, had already been named as amongst those who were to sit upon the court-martial appointed to try the culprit.

"Gad! the fellow has done for himself *now*, and no mistake!" Captain Bullock, the captain in question, exclaimed gleefully. "Couldn't have managed it better if he had tried for a century, d—— him! None of your half measures, praise the stars! Court-martial to-day, sentence to-morrow, hanged the day after! That's your style, gentlemen, and I only wish we could rattle off the rest of the rascals in the same fashion!"

"But, goodness gracious me! Do I understand you, Captain Bullock?" Lady Ballybrophy exclaimed, dropping her egg-spoon in her consternation. "Mr. Kennedy of Mount Kennedy —Mr. Kennedy, our nearest neighbour!— our—— Me lord! Me lord, d'ye hear? Oh my goodness gracious! Me lord! *Me lord!* Are you listening, me lord?"

"'Pon honour, your la'ship, if I'd ha' guessed your la'ship 'ud ha' taken it so, 'pon honour I'd ha' held my tongue about the matter," Captain Bullock replied in rather crestfallen tones. "But I never dreamt your la'ship would interest yourself in such a fellow. Why, he's known and cited all over the county of C—— for a common firebrand! Every one has heard of the way he spoke of Colonel B——; your la'ship sure knows all about *that?* And think too of the example! Why, d—— it all— begging your la'ship's pardon—those turf-and-buttermilk rascals would never have had the impudence to lift their noses if 't hadn't been for fellows like this Kennedy—a gentleman born, curse him!—condoling with them, and talking up and down the country about their treatment. Their *treatment!* Why the very expression is treasonable, and so I'm sure my lord will say!"

But my lord said nothing. The news had shocked Lord Ballybrophy beyond all power of speaking. With that rapid revulsion to a half-forgotten sentiment of which even well-balanced minds are capable under strong emotion, he suddenly felt all his old affection for his former friend spring up again within him at the news of his appalling peril. Making an excuse for leaving the room, he spent the whole of the rest of that day pacing to and fro in his study, a prey to the liveliest anxiety, now and then sending to C—— Courthouse to find out how the case was proceeding, and what the chances were of a favourable verdict.

He was not long kept in suspense. The next day but one came the news that the court-martial's proceedings had been quite as rapid and unhesitating as Captain Bullock had predicted, and that its sentence was—*Death!* Lord Ballybrophy suffered horribly. Had he been instrumental himself in that result he could hardly have felt it more. After a sleepless night, he ordered his horse early the next morning and galloped off ten miles to the house of the Lord-Lieutenant of the county, a nobleman who, as the master of many votes, had no small influence with the powers that were. Here, by dint of vehement entreaties, he induced him to bestir himself actively, and both gentlemen besieged the gates of mercy, so as to try to obtain, if not a reversal of the sentence, at least a postponement of it.

Unfortunately they found those gates doubly and trebly barred against their efforts. Lord Camden, the Lord-Lieutenant, whose tenure of office was just then ending, was himself at his wit's end with alarm and conflicting rumours. Lord Ballybrophy went to Dublin, and saw him, but the interview proved utterly barren of results. His Excellency regretted the affair; was quite willing to admit the severity of the sentence; Mr. Kennedy, he had heard, was a

gentleman of the utmost amiability in private
life—so, for that matter, were many of the
leaders in this atrocious rebellion. He would
have been truly glad for the sake of the family
to have been able to show mercy, but really
examples, you know, examples were terribly
wanted ! The condition of the country was
shocking ; the seeds of disaffection spreading
daily. And it had been reported to him by the
military authorities that an example of this sort
would be sure to have a great, and an immediately good effect.

In vain Lord Ballybrophy pointed out that,
as Mr. Kennedy was not a rebel, to hang him
could hardly produce any particular effect one
way or other upon those that were. His
Excellency, as a matter of politeness, admitted
the argument, but clung all the same tenaciously
to his position. If Mr. Kennedy was not a
rebel, then probably he was a United Irishman ;
or if he was not a United Irishman, then he was
certain to be tainted with dangerous principles
of some sort, or he would never have used the
offensive language he had about officers commanding in the C—— district. In short, his case
was clearly not one of those in which the arms
of justice could with any safety be shortened.

While Lord Ballybrophy was thus inconveniencing officials in Dublin, Mrs. Kennedy had been similarly engaged upon the spot. It had come to her knowledge that several important witnesses upon her husband's side —Protestant witnesses, and persons of the most unblemished loyalty—had been refused admittance to the court by the sentries on guard upon the day of the trial, and, armed with this apparently irresistible plea for delay, she presented herself boldly before General H——, by whom the fatal sentence would have to be confirmed.

The conversation which took place on this occasion is so short, and has been so well authenticated, that it seems worth setting it down in full.

Upon finding herself in the great man's presence, Mrs. Kennedy lost no time, but at once entered a protest against the sentence, so hastily passed, being carried into execution.

" And pray, madam," exclaimed the General impatiently, " what grounds have you for asking for any delay ? "

The poor lady might perhaps have answered with truth that she had a good many grounds, but being, as it appears, a person of unusually strong practical sense, she contented herself with stating briefly what has been said above about

K

the refusal of the sentries to admit her husband's witnesses into court.

"Good God, madam! Are you certain of what you are stating there?" her hearer exclaimed, with some dismay.

"I am perfectly certain, sir," she replied, quietly, "and can prove it upon the oaths of the Prevented."

With that she put her hand into her pocket, and proceeded to read aloud a deposition attested upon oath by one of the said Prevented. Unfortunately, before she had got to the bottom of the first page an orderly rushed in with an important dispatch. General H—— read it, muttered a hasty apology, and rushed from the room. Mrs. Kennedy never saw him again.

Whether upon reconsidering the matter he felt that it would be ungentlemanlike to "go behind" his subordinates; whether time pressed, and it was too troublesome to go over the same ground twice, or whether the crowning necessity of an "example" forced his hand, whatever the cause may have been, it is certain that no delay *did* take place. On the contrary, the sentence was rigorously carried out the very next day, down to its last grim detail, at the termination of which ceremonial Eustace Kennedy's head was set up upon the spikes of C—— jail almost within view of his own drawing-room windows. One relaxation must be recorded. By a special act of grace his Excellency Lord Camden desired that what remained of the criminal—not his head, which was otherwise required—should be restored to the widow, to be interred as she thought fit; if indeed she could discover any clergyman bold enough to utter Christian rites over so scandalous an offender.

Lord Ballybrophy took the matter very badly. He could not get it out of his mind. Day and night he was haunted by the thought of Eustace Kennedy. Now he reproached himself that he had not flung aside all decorum and openly supported his poor friend in the dock; now, that he had ever allowed that foolish quarrel to grow up, which had robbed the latter at a critical time of his own priceless advice; again, that he had not at' least exchanged a last melancholy handshake with poor Eustace in C—— jail. No amount of self-argument; no amount of knowledge that the deceased had brought it upon himself—if not by what he was accused of, at least by a disregard of his own interests which amounted to a crime—all this was of no avail. The sight of the two officers who had served upon the court-martial became like poison to him. He could not eat with

their detested faces opposite.   His food did
him no good.   Even steady drinking—the
usually infallible comfort and refuge of his
age—brought him no perceptible relief.   He
wandered incessantly through his grounds, and
about the deer-park; fixing his eyes now upon
Mount Kennedy House, now upon its churchyard, now again upon the distant landscape; at
which point he would suddenly avert his eyes
with a horribly vivid realization of what was
at that moment to be seen upon the top of
C—— jail, the walls of which even at this
distance were perceptible between the last big
pair of oaks.

   It was in this uncomfortable condition of
mind that we found him upon the evening
selected to take up this little history, and which
was only separated by a few days from the
events above recorded.   Ever since dinner he
had been wandering about—he knew not himself why or whither—feeling only that it was
impossible for him to return to the house and
to take up his own ordinary and dignified *rôle*
in life.   The sun sank.   The night fell.   A
moon began to twinkle upon the grass, and to
illuminate the bracken, but still Lord Ballybrophy lingered.   His thoughts were in the
past ; his mind kept going over and over again

scenes in which he and Eustace Kennedy had taken part. Even his friend's faults; that unfortunate "laxity" of his; his easy-going ways; his lack of personal dignity; the ridiculous indulgence he had always shown to his inferiors; all these were forgotten; irradiated by that light which Death is apt to confer upon those who have passed beyond the reach of our most vigilant criticism.

Suddenly, as he stood gazing across the park, now white as paper in the moonlight, a figure crossed the plane of his vision. It was a very odd-looking figure—odd enough to have caused a superstitious mind to take it for one of those familiar gnomes or elderly pixies known as "cluricans," and famous in Irish fairy lore as the bearers of bags or purses which, if seized at the right moment, will render their captor rich ever after beyond the dreams of misers. Like the clurican, the figure in question moreover carried a bag, which it seemed to be anxious to conceal from observation, for every now and then it paused, peered cautiously round it, and again proceeded slowly and laboriously on its way.

Lord Ballybrophy was not superstitious—certainly not in so ignorant a fashion as this—and it did not occur to him to suspect the

figure he was looking at of being anything so
vulgar as a fairy. For all that he eyed it
with considerable suspicion, as indeed was only
natural; the times not being so safe or so
simple that unaccounted-for figures could be
allowed to prowl as they pleased across a
gentleman's private deer-park.

Suddenly he recognized it. It was that
rascally old poacher, and progenitor of poachers,
Thady O'Roon, the original, the utterly con-
temptible cause of the quarrel between himself
and poor Eustace Kennedy!

A flood of angry recollections poured across
his mind at the remembrance. But for that
miserable old creature who knows but what they
might never have quarrelled? Who knows but
what his friend might at that moment be alive?

"Poaching again too!" he exclaimed aloud.
"And poor Eustace that so believed in their
gratitude!"

Why he should have felt the offence of
poaching to be an especial insult to Eustace's
memory, seeing that when alive he had never
shown any adequate sense of its enormity, he
could not have explained. It was not strictly
logical, but then, our emotions are often not
strictly logical. Anyhow the event gave a fresh
turn to the current of Lord Ballybrophy's

thoughts, which so far was a benefit. He started off, and ran actively down the grass, which here lay at a considerable slope, calling as he did so in commanding tones to the poacher to stop.

Instead of doing anything of the sort, the old fellow, after a violent start, ran on all the faster in the direction in which he was going, which would take him in a few minutes out of the deer-park into that triangular-shaped piece of wood of which mention has already several times been made.

Lord Ballybrophy followed hotly. If he had paused to consider the matter, perhaps the lateness of the hour, combined with a sense of his own dignity, might have hindered his doing so. As it was, he did not pause to consider. The most elementary of all instincts, the instinct of the hunter, was aroused, and to run the old rascal down, to take his bag from him, and, if its contents proved to be what he expected, to pack him off that night to C—— jail, became an imperative necessity.

The wood being a small one, by the time he had got into it old Thady was already clambering over the fence at the further end, which led, it may be remembered, into the Mount Kennedy churchyard. Lord Ballybrophy followed, tearing his hands badly as he did so

upon one of his own elaborately contrived
defences, and nearly losing his hat and wig,
which caught in an overhanging bough. Once
in the clearer space he flattered himself that
he should have no difficulty in running the
culprit to earth.

To his surprise he found himself mistaken.
When he got into the churchyard the moonlight was filling the whole of it, but not a
sign of old Thady or of his bag was to be
seen. With an activity that astonished himself,
and which was probably due to the state of
excitement he had been in all the evening, Lord
Ballybrophy followed up the search with all the
zest of a school-boy. Sword in hand he explored
the bushes, the briars, every corner of the enclosed space. His feet got entangled in the
grass, which grew long and rank, as its wont
is in churchyards; the few upright stones threw
weird and goblin-like shadows upon the ground;
the moonlight was broken and baffling, but still
he persevered. He knew that the old rascal
must be somewhere close at hand, and with
that fact before his mind was resolved not to
leave the spot till he had secured him.

Suddenly he caught sight of him curled like
a scared rabbit behind one of the upright stones !
With a whoop of satisfaction, hardly to have

been expected from such dignified lips, he pounced upon him, clutched him by the neck, and dragged him into the open moonlight.

"Why you old——! You—you—you——" Lord Ballybrophy was too much out of breath at the moment to think of any sufficiently scathing terms of abuse, indeed he was not at any time an eloquent nobleman. As for the culprit, he appeared to be struck idiotic from sheer dismay. A scrubby old red wig which had covered his head had fallen awry in the scuffle, and under it his bald poll glistened in the moonlight. He wore an old-fashioned livery coat, which hung in flaps about his thighs; his breeches were torn; his knees knocked one against the other; his wrinkled face was of a dull yellow hue; his eyes seemed to be half-sunken with apprehension. In short it is impossible to imagine a more ridiculous, and at the same time a more suspicious-looking figure.

Meanwhile the bag, which was the most important element in the matter, was quietly reposing behind the tombstone, where it had been left by its bearer. Lord Ballybrophy picked it up, still retaining his grasp upon old Thady, and turned to leave the churchyard. His first impulse was to march both culprits up to the "Great House." On second thoughts, however, it struck him that it would be better to burden himself only with the live one, leaving the other where it was, and where it could be sent for at any moment.

The flat-topped slab of another tombstone caught his eye at this juncture, and suggested itself as a suitable place upon which to institute a sort of preliminary examination. If the contents of the bag proved, as he felt certain they would prove, to be a hare or a rabbit, in that case he would pack old Thady off that very night without further formalities to C—— jail, to await his turn at the next assizes.

It was not without some sense of derogation that he decided to institute this preliminary examination with his own hands. Still, having achieved the whole affair single-handed so far, he felt a natural pride in bringing it single-handed to a conclusion. Accordingly he picked up the bag, and carried it to the tombstone, retaining his hold upon old Thady, who indeed offered no resistance, but allowed himself to be dragged like a piece of inert matter in the grip of his capturer. Evidently something very hard and solid was at the bottom of the bag ; harder and more solid than Lord Ballybrophy could account for under the circumstances. An indescribable reluctance overtook him as he was about to plunge his hand into it ; instead therefore of doing so, he simply lifted the weighted end, and tilted it a little forward so as to allow the contents to roll over on to the smooth, flat surface of the tombstone.

Over they rolled sure enough ; further ; further still ; over and over—certainly something very round and very hard was in that bag ! Something too—very—very—" Why ?—What ? What ? What ?—" Lord Ballybrophy's eyes began to start out of their sockets ; his hair to rise up stiff and bristling under his wig ; his blood, first to coagulate, and then to seem to be rushing like a tide of red-hot lava through his veins. The next moment a succession of piercing shrieks startled the card-players at the other end of the park. Pell-mell, out they rushed ; the officers first, the chaplain next, the ladies last, the latter gathering their skirts around them. Once in the deer-park they stared helplessly here and there, not knowing where to turn, or in what direction to look for the cause of their alarm. They were guided at last to the right place by the apparition of a little old man, leaping, gesticulating, and running wildly to and fro in front of the churchyard. There, flat upon the grass, apparently in a swoon, they found

Lord Ballybrophy. His hat had fallen in one
direction, his wig in another, his sword was
below him, and immediately above him, upon
the smooth flat slab of the tombstone, and looking as white and placid in the moonlight as if it
had merely formed part of some monumental
effigy, lay—the head of Eustace Kennedy !

How had it got there? and what under the
circumstances was now to be done with it? were
two questions, which—the first attentions to the
sick man having been paid—not a little exer-
cised the minds of those who were the witnesses
of the foregoing rather remarkable scene. As
regards the first question it was easily answered,
old Thady O'Roon making no secret of having
himself stolen it that very afternoon from the
spikes of C—— jail, where the majesty of the
law had impaled it. "Bedad an' I thought maybe the poor mhaster might slape aisier t'home,"
seemed to be the only explanation he was capable of giving when called upon to account for
so startling a piece of larceny. As regards the
second question—well, in the end the head was
allowed to rest peacefully enough not far from
where it then lay, with the remainder of the poor
clay thereunto appertaining. The truth was,
that once the first blush of their zeal was a little
abated, the authorities, civil as well as military,

were not eager to allow too dazzling a blaze of publicity to fall upon all their recent proceedings. So successful indeed were they in this administrative modesty, that to this day the foregoing transaction is rarely alluded to, and to the best of my belief is known to but few, and those few chiefly the descendants of the actual partakers in it.

Lord Ballybrophy, the reader will be glad to hear, recovered in due time from his attack, and lived to a good old age, respected by all who knew him. The Kennedy family soon afterwards quitted Mount Kennedy. The property was let upon a long grazing lease. The house was shut up, and so by degrees fell into that condition of neglect and decay in which we now see it. With regard to old Thady O'Roon, about whom I specially inquired, my friend could give me no further information.

FAMINE ROADS AND FAMINE
MEMORIES

I⊤ has sometimes seemed to me as if every great event, especially if it be of the more tragic order, ought to have some distinctive cairn or monument of its own; some spot at which one could stand, as before a shrine, there to meditate upon it, and upon it alone. Such a shrine—though only in my own eminently private mental chapel—the great Irish Famine of 1846-47 possesses, and has possessed for more years than I can now readily reckon. Whenever I think of it there rises before me one particular spot, in one particular corner of Connemara; one particular cluster of cabins, or rather wrecks of cabins, for roofs there have been none since I knew it first. There they stand, those poor perishing memorials, and yearly the nettles spread a little further across their hearthstones, and yearly the slope on

which they rest crumbles a little nearer to the
sea, and yearly the rain batters them a little
more down, and the green things cluster more
closely around them, and so it will be till one
day the walls too will roll over, and the bog
from above will overtake them, and the last
trace of what was once a populous village will
have disappeared, without so much as a *Hic
Jacet* to say where it stood.

To get to this very private chapel you must
not mind rough walking, neither must you mind
trespassing ; indeed that last is a mere English
fetish, to which the freer-hearted Celt has never
been a slave. Leaving the village of Leenane—
it stands, as you are probably aware, upon the
south shore of the Greater Killary—you keep
straight on till you come to a certain white gate
on the right hand side of the road. Turn in here
—you are trespassing already, but never mind,
there are no notice boards—and you will find
yourself upon a grass-grown roadway, with the
shining level of the fiord below, and above a
steep incline of bog, cutting across the sky ;
a sky which may be friendly at the moment,
or may be threatening, but which is sure to be
a sky alive with clouds ; clouds which are never
for a moment at rest ; clouds of every form,
and of every degree of transitoriness, but each

one of which has its own separate make and semblance, unlike any cloud—had we eyes to perceive that difference—that ever was or ever will be in any sky again.

"What I really dislike about the west of Ireland is its dreadful dampness and darkness!" says the tourist. Since you say so, oh tourist!— lord of our destiny, our master and our patron —why it must be so, and from your decisions there can be no appeal. Otherwise—if I dared for an instant to contest so great an authority —I should be disposed to say that this particular walk, and I could match it with others, has always stood out before my mind as one of the brightest things I am acquainted with in this not particularly bright world of ours.

Even to think of it at a distance, and amongst other surroundings, is to think of something so transcendently bright that, in the momentary confusion of the mental picture, it seems—though of course quite absurdly—as if there were something spiritually, rather than merely corporeally, luminous about that extraordinary brightness.

And yet it is not from the side of the Killary —gleaming lane of water though it is—that this sense of light comes chiefly. The Killary, like other fiords, is the prisoner of its own mountains. North and south of it, but especially north, they peer continually down upon it, and rarely fail in any gleam to see their own bald pates accurately presented for their inspection. It is on the other side of our roadway, where the mountains stand further back, and where we have the free hillside for our foreground, that this sense of light is so strong, and so all-pervading.

Walking along it one seems to grow fairly intoxicated with light. To look suddenly upwards is to skate and skim away across a succession of magic mirrors—a thing scarce the bravest eyes dare adventure. Every boulder —and you may reckon them by tens of thousands—offers you a separate mirror, a separate opal or diamond-becrusted shield.

And not after rain only. These jewels are not evanescent ones; things to dry up and disappear after a shower. On the contrary, they belong to the boulders; are their own absolute heritage, and family regalia. Mica and talc, schist, and hornblende—things jewel-like in effect, if not in value—these make up the sum and substance of these masses from the Maam Turk and Bennaboola ranges.

Do you care to see whence they came? If so you have only to turn to where the foreground dips a little. There! see that single glittering peak, cutting the sky-line like a knife, and naked as an iceberg. That is the "Diamond," and for once the English name, if undistinguished enough, is at least reasonably descriptive. It stands above Kylemore lake, and is rather more brilliant than the other mountains, its neighbours, simply because it is rather steeper.

The natural history of these mountains of Connemara—Iar Connaught, to give the region its proper title—is at first a little puzzling. The readiest way to understand it is to imagine yourself upon the top of one of those mountains opposite—Mweelrea will do as well as another, —and having done so, to look first seaward, afterwards landward; to the north, to the east, to the south, and so west again, until by degrees the whole plan and make of the region begins to rise up clear before your mind.

Your first impression in that case would probably be a very definite one. You would perceive the general effect to be as if the sky had recently been dropping lakes upon the land, and the land on its side had been showering rocks upon the sea. Westward, where the two great promontories of Augrus and Slyne Head jut into the sea, you would perceive, between their

outstretched points, to right and to left of
them, and far out over the sea, a multitude of
island points, dark above, gleaming and glittering where the sun catches upon their wave-
washed sides. Some of these islands are gathered
into clusters ; others are single, or in scattered
groups. There are round islands, long islands,
oblong islands; islands of every shape and size,
from the tiny illauns and carrigeens, which
barely afford a foothold to the passing gull, up
to the respectable-sized islands of Inishbofin and
Inishturk, which boast their populations of five
and six hundred inhabitants apiece, and carry
on, or until lately did carry on, a considerable
traffic in kelp, receiving in return *poteen*, and
such other necessaries of life as are not to be
found upon the islands.

Turning now in imagination from the sea,
and looking inland, you perceive the same sort
of general effect, only that here the elements are
reversed. The sea here has everywhere invaded
and taken possession of the land. If you tried
to follow one of its glittering arms to its end,
when you thought you had seen the last of it,
you would find it re-appearing on the other side
of some small summit, and winding away in
intricate curves and convolutions far as the eye
could see. As for the lakes, they are endless,

bewildering; past all power of man to count or
to remember. With all the Celt's talent for
bestowing appropriate names upon the objects
with which he found himself surrounded, here
nature seems to have been too much for him;
a large proportion of these lakes having no
names at all. Even to know them apart is sufficiently perplexing. Lough Inagh and Derry-
clare, with their wooded islands; Ballinahinch,
with its castle and its salmon streams; Kylemore, with its modern splendours; Lough Muck
and Lough Fee, filling up the gorge which
stretches seaward between two steep cliffs;
these, and perhaps a dozen more, we may distinguish readily enough; but who will undertake to give an account of the endless multitude
of loughs and lougheens which stud the whole
face of the country between Lough Corrib and
the sea?

Turn now to the lower ground. You might
compare it to a looking-glass starred with cracks,
the cracks standing for the ground, the inter-
mediate spaces for the lakes! Many of these
lakes lie far out of every one's reach, and are
never seen at all, or only once in a while by
some turf-cutter, on his way to a distant bog,
or some sportsman taking a fresh cast in hopes
of coming upon the pack of grouse which is re-

ported to have been seen in this direction. Other lakes again lie high up on the mountain sides, often close to the summit, where they are still less likely to be seen, though any one who will take the trouble of clambering in search of them will find his pains rewarded. Most striking of these are the so-called " corries "—bowl-shaped hollows, for the most part cut out of the solid rock. Often a whole series of such corries may be seen lying parallel to one another upon the vertical sides of precipices, some containing water, others again dry. When full they are usually partly formed of drift, which accumulating at the mouth of the hollow, hinders the water from escaping. As for their origin, ask a local geologist, and he will tell you that they are due to direct ice action, and chiefly for the following reasons. First, that they differ entirely from hollows made by other agencies ; secondly, that nothing in the least resembling them is now being formed by the sea ; thirdly, that they cannot be due to the ordinary meteoric agents—rain, snow, wind, running water, and so forth—since those very agents are at present engaged in smoothing them away. Only after this be very careful not to put the same question to any other geologist, since he will most likely supply you with the following facts. First, that other agents besides ice are perfectly capable of making similar hollows ; secondly, that the sea is at this very moment engaged in scooping out small coves, which if raised in a general elevation of the land, would in time present a similar appearance ; thirdly, that the chief agent must have been not ice, but faults and dislocations in the rock, aided subsequently by glacial or marine action. Then your mind will be disturbed, as mine has been. Where experts differ to such an extent, how, it may be asked, is the mere ignorant inquirer to steer his modest course ?

But these are high matters. Our walk in life is a different, and a lowlier one. Returning for a moment to our roadway, we presently leave it, and pass across a long stretch of bog, up one incline, and down another, over a stream —how I hardly know, for the last time I went that way there were no stepping-stones—and now we have reached the point for which we set out. We have arrived at our ruined village. We are standing upon the *Famine Road.*

Certain words and certain combinations of words seem to need an eminently local education in order adequately to appreciate them. These two words, "Famine road," are amongst the number. To other, larger minds than ours they are probably without any particular meaning or inwardness. To the home-staying Irishman or Irishwoman they mean only too much. To hear them casually uttered is to be penetrated by a sense of something at once familiar and terrible. The entire history of two of the most appalling years that any country has ever been called upon to pass through seems to be summed up, and compendiously packed into them.

Other mementoes of the famine, besides its roads, exist, of course, in Ireland. As his train lounges through its flat central counties the intelligent stranger must have more than once observed some erratic-looking obelisk, or other odd development of the art of the builder. If he bestirs himself to inquire what it is, he will be pretty certain to be told that it is a " Famine work,"—as though bad architecture and empty stomachs had a natural connection ! There are plenty of such abortive " Famine works " scattered over the country, but the Famine roads were the official ones ; the ones longest persisted in, and in the vast majority of cases, alas ! they were the most absolutely futile and abortive of all.

Do not let the word *road* mislead you though. Road, as is plain to be seen, there is none here, nor has been for a long time back. For some

years after the Famine, fifteen or sixteen perhaps, for the grass here is not very quick-
growing, a road of some sort survived. Nay,
I have even been assured that a spirited-minded
gentleman once undertook to drive his coach
along this part of the edge of the shore, up
to the top of the ridge, and so down by the
Devil's Gap to Salrock. If he did do so,
and survived the entertainment, that divinity
that watches over the doings of madmen and
drunkards must assuredly have sat upon the
coach-box beside him on that occasion.
Whether the tale be true or false, it is at
least certain that for a few years a road of
some sort existed. After that the mountain
took it back to its own green bosom, and, save
that it survives as a line of exceptional wetness,
and that after prolonged rains it reappears in the
form of an odd-looking trough or shallow canal,
there is no more sign that a road ever ran here
than there was when Saint Patrick preached
upon Croaghpatrick yonder, or when Saint
Fechin paddled past the point of Renvyle to
take up his abode upon the sea-scourged rocks
of Ard Oilen.

If the Famine road has disappeared, however, other traces of the famine, or rather of the
pre-famine condition of things, are still to be

seen. Only if you have eyes to see them though, and if the indications—worn almost to invisibility by this time—are sufficiently familiar to make themselves felt as you look around you. Turning towards the higher ground you can count a succession of small humps or projections along the top of the ridge. There is one with a gable end still visible to help the reckoning. Fifty years back those projections were all villages, or groups, at any rate, of from three to ten cabins. In those pre-famine days the rural population throughout Ireland was all but incredibly dense. The fact that nearly four hundred thousand one-roomed cabins are stated by the Registrar-General to have disappeared between the census before and after the Famine, is alone sufficiently indicative of the change. Of such one-roomed cabins these villages probably all consisted. They were apparently unconnected with one another, even by a "bohereen," yet this now utterly vacant hillside must have hummed in those days with life, and been as busy with its comings and goings as any village green.

Throughout Connemara decent roads were unknown up to the beginning of this century, and even well within that period they were practically non-existent. I can put my hand at this moment upon a bundle of letters describing a visit paid to the Martins of Ballinahinch, somewhere about the middle of the thirties. From the neighbourhood of Tuam the visitor drove to the ferry beyond Headford; crossed it in a very leaky boat—as in fact you do still—found mountain ponies which had been sent by her hosts to meet her upon the other side; rode up-hill and down-hill across some thirty miles of heathery track, and so down to Ballinahinch to pay her visit.

Out of this roadless condition it emerged rather suddenly. The roads over which the tourist of to-day travels, and which are excellent, were all carried out by one enterprising road-maker not long before the Famine. Outlying villages such as these naturally lay beyond the reach of such central highways, and had to be left to nature. Imagine how urgently some way of connecting them with one another and with the outside world must have been wished for, how badly they must have been wanted—*until made*. Then the need for such means of communication ceased suddenly, and has never returned. Thus the whole irony of the Famine roads stands revealed in a sentence.

The mere bald enumeration of the number

of lives extinguished in this one county of Galway during those two years of famine is enough to make one ask oneself how any man or woman living there at the time retained his or her sanity. Many did not. The list of those, well above the reach of actual hunger, who broke down, mind and body alike, from mere pressure upon their vital forces, from pity, from a sense of unutterable horror, is greater than would be believed, or than has ever been set down in print. And can anybody reasonably wonder? Take the mere official reports; the report, for instance, of one county inspector in this very district, and you will find him speaking of a hundred and fifty bodies picked up by himself and his assistants along a single stretch of road. Multiply this fiftyfold, and ask yourself what that means?

And if upon the roadsides, what of the less easily attainable places? Think of the thousands of solitary cabins and sheilings high on the hillsides? Think of the little congeries of similar cabins, such as these whose wrecks lie around us here; of the groups collected round their hearths, so large at first, growing smaller and smaller day by day, until none were left to carry out the dead. Think of the eyes lifted to heaven here upon these very slopes on which we are to-day indolently strolling. Think of the separate hell gone through by each individual father and mother of all that starving multitude.   And when all hope was over, when the bitter draught was almost drunk, the end had almost come, that end which must have been so welcome, because there were none left to live for, think of the lying down to watch the vanishing away of this familiar green landscape in the last grey mists of death.

Unhappily we are not driven to piece out such scenes from the shallows of our own moral consciousness, and fifty years after the event. Would that we were ! The most matter-of-fact, the most coldly official reports of the time read like the imaginings of some brain-sick poet; to turn over the leaves of your *Hansard* is like dropping upon the pool of Malebolge.   In a speech in the House of Commons Mr. Horsman—not, I take it, an imaginative orator—speaks, for instance, of the condition of Ireland as follows : " It is like a country devastated by an enemy ; like a country which the destroying angel has swept over. . . . The population struck down, the air a pestilence, the fields a solitude, the chapels deserted, the priest and the pauper famishing together; no inquests; no rites; no record even of the dead; the high-road

a charnel-house; the land a chaos; a ruined pro-
prietary, a panic-struck tenantry, the soil un-
tilled, the workhouse a pest. Death, desolation,
despair reigning throughout the land." [1]

Although there had been warnings in abundance, yet the suddenness with which the blow
finally fell seems to have reduced people and
rulers alike to apathy. Every account agrees
as to this suddenness. Old people to this
day speak of it as of a very thunder-clap of
destiny. Again and again I have had described
to me the evening of the great Blight. How
warm the preceding months had been. How
promising the potato crop had appeared. For
years it had been dwindling, but this year all
the old abundance seemed to have returned.
Every face smiled; last year's scarcity and
partial famine was forgotten; the little children
gathered bunches of the detestable violet-and-
white flowers, and ran laughing along the roads
with them. Suddenly something happened.
There came a day of steaming mist, and that
evening a scent of decay was perceptible all
over the country. And next morning when
the people rose up the Plague was over the
land. North, south, east, and west—especially
west—a cry went up that the potatoes had

_____
[1] *Hansard,* 3rd series, vol. iv. p. 609.

rotted. Eight millions of people—say six, say five, so as to include only those absolutely dependent upon that miserable tuber —and nothing but rotting abominations, unfit for pigs, between them and a cruel death.

Here was the situation, and how was it met? We had better not ask, seeing that the answer to that question brings us face to face with about as lamentable an example of the art of blundering as any that the records of our poor blunder-ridden race can afford. How far the Government—misfortunate abstraction!— did or did not realize the extent of the disaster, is a point which may be disputed till the crack of doom. That it did not act as if it had realized it, and that the earlier steps which it took to mitigate it were about as ineffective as could have been devised, few have ever been brave enough to deny. That the blame must be shared amongst other impersonal potentates —Circumstance, Environment, Fate, and so forth—is true. Still, when we have admitted this, what then? Even that colder-blooded type of philosopher who is disposed to regard a disaster of the kind as a natural, if lamentable, remedy for an otherwise incurable disease, will surely admit that to save life is for any civil-

ized government the first and most elementary
of all its duties?

This, however, it is about time to remember,
is a volume of tales, and *not* a political sermon.
Turning over that wallet of odds and ends
which all tale-tellers are supposed, consciously
or unconsciously, to carry about with them, I
find nothing that seems to me at all likely to
serve as even the tiniest pebble of a contribution
to this tremendous national cairn. One story
indeed comes back to my memory, but it has
the double defect of not belonging to the actual
time, and of being laid within the limits of a
class upon which the effect of the Famine was
indirect rather than direct. Such as it is, however, and for lack of better, it must serve.
There are themes, moreover, before which even
the studied audacity of the story-teller shrinks
back, and would as soon not be called upon
to encounter. In itself the story in question
seemed to me, at least when I heard it, to be
worth recording. The situation is surely an
odd one; indeed, under any circumstances less
destructive of all the ordinary conventions of
existence, might fairly have been pronounced
impossible. Here, as will presently be seen,
was a young girl; well born, beautiful; brought
up in all the easy-going luxury of a large

country-house; reduced nevertheless to a state of destitution as complete as that of any nameless waif or stray in one of our cities ; dependent for her daily bread upon the charity of a couple of old servants; without a friend to inquire after her, or a soul to take the smallest interest in her future. So completely had she been abandoned by every one, that her choice, as my informant assured me, lay literally between accepting the hand of a man who was not her equal in any sense of the word, and who, moreover, had only his own thews and sinews to depend upon, or—the workhouse.

If the reader cares to know how this story of Eleanor d'Arcy and her two lovers came to be told to me, that is a very simple matter. I was staying a few years ago in a country-house, not in the west of Ireland, but in its more prosaic midlands. By some accident we got talking one evening after dinner about the Famine, and first one person and then another related some circumstance connected with it, which report, or some fragment of family tradition, had chanced to bring within their memory. Since none of our memories extended to the actual time, there was, however, a perceptible flavour of vagueness about these impressions, and it was perhaps from a realization of this fact that our talk by and by drifted to more contemporary matters, and the great Irish Famine was for the time forgotten.

Later in the evening an old gentleman— not an Irishman; a rich man, and usually held to be a somewhat crabbed one — crossed the room, and took a chair not far from where I was sitting. We were rather friends, as one counts friendships with people whom one only meets in other people's houses, and upon this occasion he seemed more disposed to be confidential than usual. He had not said anything during the recent discussion, and we now talked on for some time about things in general. Suddenly he interrupted me in the middle of a sentence.

"You were talking a while ago about the Irish Famine," he said abruptly. "I was in Ireland myself at the time, at least soon afterwards, in 1848. I did not care to talk about it just now, but if you would like to hear what I saw and did, you are welcome. It is an old story, and I don't suppose any one, except myself, remembers a single word about it. Stop me, by the way, if I grow tedious. It's the fashion of us old fellows, you know, when we get talking about the past."

Naturally I expressed a lively desire to hear

M

what he had to tell me, and further suggested that as the rest of the party seemed to have drifted away, out of doors, or it was not very clear where, he and I might without incivility betake ourselves to a certain inner room, which I had before marked as a desirable refuge, and where we should be certain not to be disturbed.

To this he agreed, and we settled ourselves in a couple of arm-chairs, telling the servants that we would be responsible for the lamps, and that no one was to disturb us. These arrangements made, I folded my hands in my lap, and prepared to listen.

AFTER THE FAMINE

Oh, never let one leaf on thee be grown!
All brown, all naked let thy fields be shown,
Where they, thy children, sleep beneath the sky;
So thick, dear God, *how* thick their fresh graves lie!
They were thy children, and they loved thee well,
Thou wert their mother, and a fiend of hell.
Be barren henceforth! Let not one leaf show,
To mock that hapless dust so late laid low.

I

WE sat for some time silently, each of us in
our respective arm-chair. My old gentleman
did not seem to be in any hurry to begin his
story. On the contrary he appeared to have
lapsed into a contemplative mood, and to have
practically forgotten my existence. At last he
looked up, and caught my eye.

"I have been thinking," he said, smiling at
the look of impatience which I managed to throw
into it, "how odd it is, the way in which some

impressions seem always to remain extraordinarily fresh and vivid, while others, which ought, one would think, to be much more permanent, fade away entirely, and disappear. I suppose I have seen and done as much as my neighbours, and yet if you were to ask me to give you the details of any of the more important events of my life, I doubt if I could remember a single one of them. Whereas this incident, which I am going to tell you about, and which, as far as I am concerned, had no permanent effects whatever, has always remained just as vivid as it was at the first. Especially when I find myself in Ireland, it seems as if it must all have happened only yesterday, and I can hardly per-suade myself that nearly fifty years have passed since then. It seems as if I were still at Castle d'Arcy, and still looking out at the——But stop! this won't do. That is not the right way to begin. I had better go back, and tell you the whole story from the start, or I shall never get it straight.

" My reasons for going to Ireland, I must begin by explaining, were not a bit philan-thropical, still less political ; they were entirely practical and financial. I had lately joined the firm to which I still belong, and my partners and myself had a large sum of money that had to be

invested in land, and at that time there was an
enormous quantity of Irish land to be had at
excessively low prices, having been forced into
the market by the orders of the Encumbered
Estates court.   It having been decided that the
sum in question should be invested in Irish
land, the only question that remained was what
land we were to select for the purpose.   I was
the youngest of the firm, and the other two
insisted therefore that I should go to Ireland
to explore.   One of the properties offered to
us was in the County Galway, in a very remote corner of it, upon the shores of Cashla
Bay.   It looked an enormous territory upon
paper, running out into the sea, and back
to the foot of the mountains.   Its owner,
Mr. d'Arcy, had recently died, and the
creditors, who were endeavouring to sell the
estate, had offered it to us on extraordinarily
low terms.   Somehow from the first I had
not relished the errand.   I knew nothing of
Ireland.   As for Cashla Bay it might have
been in Kamscatka for anything I knew to the
contrary.   Still I knew what every one else
knew; what the newspapers had told us, and——
In short, I did not fancy the errand.   I could
not well refuse, however, and neither of my
partners showed any inclination to go in my

stead, so in the end I went. It had been
arranged that I was to sleep at the house
belonging to the property, there being, we
were told, no inns in the district; but beyond
this fact I knew nothing as to what I might
expect to find upon my arrival.

"Well, I started. There is no need to
describe my journey. It took longer than it
would do to-day, but it had already been a
good deal shortened. A railway had recently
been opened to Galway, and some twenty-two
hours from the time of my leaving London I
stood upon the platform of that town, and
looked round for some conveyance to carry
me whatever distance still remained to be
traversed.

"There was no lack of them, such as they
were. A dozen patched cars, chiefly held together apparently by pieces of string, stood
there, and at least three dozen carmen were
leaning across a wooden bar; shouting, shoving
one another, and waving arms out of tatter-
demalion coat-sleeves. I picked out the best
vehicle I could see, a fairly whole one, drawn
by a shaggy old brown mare, and driven by a
decent-looking old fellow with a mop of lint-
white hair falling on his neck, and having ascer-
tained that he knew where Castle d'Arcy was,

I got upon the car, and we proceeded upon our way.

" The famine was supposed to be over by this time, but it had left traces enough! Such scarecrows, such moving skeletons, such pitiable-looking ghosts of humanity as I passed on that drive through Galway! I am no sentimentalist, and never was, even when I was young, yet there are certain recollections connected with that drive, and with one or two others that I took during my stay that year in Ireland, which I would gladly have got rid of at the cost of a good round sum of money. However, you can imagine the details, and I need not therefore dwell upon them. We got out of Galway at last, and drove on along the coast at a monotonous jig-jog pace ; the car rattling over the stones, and the broken harness threatening at every step to give way. Being my first experience of car-driving, I clung for dear life, I remember, to a strap; my old driver meanwhile making queer chirruping noises to his horse, and now and then nodding gloomily to one or other of the passers-by.

" The distance that we drove seemed to me at the time tremendous, far greater than I had had any expectation of when I started. Most of it lay through an utterly barren region, at which I, being new to the country, stared aghast, wondering how any one out of Bedlam could possibly propose to invest money in such a God-forsaken place.   Suddenly my old Jehu, who had for some time been peering at me inquisitively across the well, turned, and speaking in that sing-song, western voice, which I that day heard for the first time, but which was soon to grow very familiar to my ear—

" ' Will it be a friend of the great d'Arcy family your 'anner is, then ? '

" I hesitated for a moment before answering. Would he upset me into the ditch, I wondered, if I told him the truth ?   Since it could not long be concealed, and since, man for man, I was certainly more than his match, I ventured to take the risk.

" ' No,' I replied, ' I don't know any of the d'Arcy family.   I was not aware in fact that any of them were left.   I have come over to look at the land, which is about to be sold.'

" My old driver turned from me as though I had been a leper, and our journey was continued in absolute silence.

" The stoniness of that country I shall never forget to my dying day.   It was not the amount of solid rock that surprised me so much as the amount of loose pieces flung about broadcast,

as if recently fallen from the sky. Mortarless
walls covered the grass like an iron network,
and in some cases heaps of stones had been
gathered together in the corners of the fields,
but, despite these efforts to dispose of them,
the stones defied collection, and lay about in
all directions. You know the sort of thing,
and can therefore easily imagine it, but to me
it was all perfectly new.

"At last, after driving some fourteen or
fifteen miles, we came to an entrance gate, which
stood wide open, and, passing through it,
entered upon a narrow road, arched over with
elms and sycamores, and through a second gate
which led us presently into a wide sweep of
park.

"The trees in this park, though wind-
blown, were larger and better grown than I
should have deemed possible, so that my eyes,
sick with the nakedness of the land through
which we had been passing, felt quite gladdened
by the aspect of at any rate former care and
cultivation which I saw around me. For
some time no dwelling-house came into sight.
The only habitation that I could see being a
sinister-looking old castle, evidently a ruin,
which stood upon the end of a jutting point.
Presently I espied another building near the

shore, not exactly a ruin, but nearly as dilapidated as one. This was a queer little round tower, perched upon the top of a hillock, having in front of it a narrow spit of grey rock, running out into the sea, and a flight of steps which led up to a revolving weather-cock which decorated its top. There was something so whimsical-looking about the whole edifice that I could not resist turning once more to my driver, and asking him what it was.

" The old fellow started, as if I had roused him from his sleep. Then he stared at the object in question, shading his eyes with his hand, so as to see it better.

" ' 'Tis indade; 'tis indade; Miss Ann's tayhouse! poor Miss Ann's tayhouse; yis indade, my God, yis indade,' he muttered, rather to himself than as if in answer to my question.

" ' And who is Miss Ann ?' asked I.

" He turned, and stared at me. ' Thar's no Miss Ann in it now at all, at all,' he replied contemptuously.

" ' Why not ?' I asked. Then as he did not answer, ' Is she dead ?' I said.

" ' Trath she *is* dead '—in a tone of the most withering contempt. ' What else would she be but dead ? 'Dade, an' 'tis them that never ought to have died that has died these times.

And 'tis only them that nobody wants that seems to be kep' alive,' he added in the same tone.

"The glance with which this last remark was accompanied gave it such an unmistakably personal application, that I made no more attempts at conversation until we reached the house.

"We came upon it in the end quite suddenly. The avenue took a sharp turn to the right, and in a minute we had stopped before the hall door. Like most houses in this part of Ireland it was built of limestone, of a rather dull grey hue. Black stains ran from the corners of most of the windows, giving it an additional aspect of neglect. The sashes of the windows were closed, and the blinds drawn down. Altogether appearances were not encouraging.

"The jangling sound of the bell pulled by my driver woke up the echoes ; then they died away, and silence once more set in. It was so still that I remember I could hear the waves breaking upon the beach below, and running back with a long sound of scraping sands and gravel.

"The old mare stood still, and steamed patiently. I took down my portmanteau from the car and waited, wondering what was going

to happen to me next. It seemed an age before
at last the sound of steps were heard approaching, apparently from a considerable distance.
Then followed a creaking of locks, the door
opened widely, and a tall, old serving-man with
a white head and stooping shoulders stood in
the aperture. He wore what seemed to have
been at one time a suit of decent livery, but
was now patched and stained, and over one
shoulder hung a frieze coat, which, big as he
was, was evidently several sizes too big for
him.

"Astonishment appeared to be his prevailing
expression. He looked at the car, and at
myself, and at the driver, as if we had all fallen
out of the moon. A word in Irish, however,
from the latter enlightened him. What that
word was I do not of course know, but never
on any human face did I see such a sudden
change of expression. A look of hatred seemed
all at once to blaze up in the old fellow's
shrivelled face as he turned it towards me. If
a glance could have killed me I should certainly have fallen dead there and then upon the
doorstep. His first impulse seemed to be to
turn, and shut that door in my face. On
second thoughts he refrained from doing this,
but stood there, scowling darkly, while the

driver and I between us carried my very moderate supply of luggage into the front hall. This done, and the car paid, and dismissed, I stood face to face with the situation.

"Evidently no offers of hospitality were to be looked for, and there was nothing for it therefore but to take the matter into my own hands.

"'Show me to a bedroom, my good man,' I said, at the same time holding out a bag for him to carry.

"'A bedroom? Ter an agus! will nothin' less than that serve thim *now!* A bedroom, wisha! My God! a bedroom!' was all the reply I got.

"Plainly the situation was one that had to be met with vigour.

"'Look here, my man,' I said firmly, 'I have come here upon business. Here I am, and here I intend to stop. Remember, too, that if I have to report any insolence upon your part it will be the worse for you. Now show me a room.'

"That I had taken the right course to ensure respect was plain. The old fellow eyed me for a moment with the glare of an enfeebled wolf; then a change passed over his face, and a peculiar look, half-contemptuous, half-deprecating, came into it. Opening a door which stood near, he begged me to 'step widin a minute till he'd

spake wi' the mistress.'   And ushering me into
a room, he departed again, before I had time to
reply.

"The room in which I found myself was a
large, and rather handsome dining-room—handsome, that is, as far as its proportions were concerned, but almost entirely empty of furniture.
In the centre stood a long table, upon which
only a single plate, knife, and fork were laid out,
although, as I immediately noticed, enough chairs
were drawn up to the table for a party of four
or five.

"It was by this time six o'clock, which at that
date was, for all but ultra-fashionables, the
ordinary dinner-hour.   I was hungry, for I had
tasted nothing since breakfast, with the exception of a very unappetizing sandwich which I
got at Mullingar.   At the moment I felt too
uneasy however to think about food.   Who
could the old fellow mean by 'the mistress'?
I asked myself.   Surely I had been told in
London that all the members of the late
owner's family were either dead, or had gone
away.   Who was she then, this mistress? and
what sort of reception was I likely under the
circumstances to find at her hands?

"I turned towards the window with a vague
thought of escape.   The gravel sweep outside

had grown hollow, and a large pool of water
had collected in the centre of it. The stillness
was intense. It was more like that of a vault
than of a house, and again a strong wish to
escape came over me. But where the deuce
was I to escape to? I could not well leap
out of the window, leaving my bag and other
possessions behind me! Besides, if I did, there
was probably no car now to be had for Galway.
No, I must stay, I decided, and face the situation
out.

"Suddenly the door behind me opened. What
sort of figure I was expecting to see I hardly
know, but certainly nothing like the one that
did come in. It was that of a young girl,
eighteen years old at most, dressed in deep
black. She came straight over towards the table,
her head bent, her hands clasped, her eyes widely
open. Suddenly she caught sight of me, and
started violently, turning as she did so, as if
inquiringly, to an old woman who followed
close at her heels, a wrinkled old creature, a
peasant apparently, or very humble retainer.

"I stood transfixed. The girl was simply the
most beautiful creature I had ever seen in my
life! Her face was very pale; the delicately-
cut mouth was half-open, and wore a piteously
beseeching expression such as one sometimes sees

in a child.   Her eyes were grey, and of an extraordinary limpidity, a limpidity that even at the first glance struck me as something absolutely new, something wholly foreign to my experience, and which even at this distance of time haunts my memory vividly.

"The look of astonishment which had come into her face on first catching sight of me remained on it, but after a moment's hesitation she bowed with a gentle, self-possessed air, the air of one to whom courtesy and hospitality come as an instinct.

"I returned her bow, very awkwardly I have no doubt, and, after another moment's hesitation, she seated herself in one of the chairs arranged round the table, not the one at the top of it; but next to the top, and a little to one side.

"'Put a plate, and knife, and fork for the gentleman, if you please, Nora,' she said in a gentle, rather sing-song voice to the old woman. 'Will you sit down here, please,'—this to me— 'they will not be long, but we have not many servants now.' This was said with a deprecating look out of those wonderful eyes of hers.

"I hesitated, abashed and conscience-stricken. Then, after a minute's hesitation, from sheer awkwardness, and from not knowing at what point to begin my explanation, I took the chair offered, which was opposite to her own, and seated myself at the table. At the same moment the door opened again, and the old man-servant entered breathlessly. Had I been in the humour to laugh I must have done so at the air of mingled horror, disgust, and fury with which he perceived me, sitting, actually sitting at table with his mistress. He began some involved explanation as to who and what I was, an explanation rendered still more incoherent by his fury, when he was seized, and all but hustled out of the room by the old woman, who literally stopped his mouth with a napkin which she carried in her hands.

"She spoke English, so that I was able to catch a word or two while she was in the act of shoving him out before her.

"'Arrah, can't you lave her in paace, you gomoral! Whist wid your tongue'—a fresh sputter of angry explanations from the old man, and another 'Whist, I tell you, whist! Lave Miss Elly alone, or I'll——' and they were gone.

"We were thus left *tête-à-tête*. I longed to speak to my companion, to apologize to her for my intrusion, but there was something about the

N

expression of her eyes, at once timid and appealing, that daunted me. I felt literally afraid of saying something that would cause them to look at me with a less friendly expression.

" The result of my hesitation was that she was the first to speak.

" ' You have come from the workhouse, have you not ? ' she said, in the same gentle, courteous tone as before, looking across the table at me as she spoke.

" I was not put more at my ease by this inquiry ! The workhouse ? Did she think I looked as if I had come out of a workhouse ? and was she in the habit of receiving people out of the workhouse to dinner ? I was too confused to do more than stammer out a denial of the imputation.

" She looked a little surprised. ' Most people who come here go first to the workhouse,' she said. ' It is at Killtoomey you know, upon the hill there. It is very full still I am told, but not quite so full as it was last year. My father went there every day until—until——' She looked suddenly towards the foot of the table with an expression of perplexity ; her face began to quiver ; her eyes to fill. I thought that she was going to cry, but after a minute's pause she rallied, and went on steadily.

" ' I have never been allowed to go there myself because of the fever, but my sisters——' This time she stopped outright, and it was with a look of something like terror that she glanced first to one side of the table, and then to the other, a look not so much of grief as of a sort of curious disbelief ; the look of a person who knows, and yet who will not know ; who cannot resolve to convince herself by actual evidence that what she fears even to think of is a fact.

" I was so terrified by this expression of hers, and so expectant of some sudden breakdown on her part, that it was with a feeling of extreme relief that I heard the footsteps of the two old creatures coming in again. They clattered forward, carrying dishes—a large handsomely embossed silver one I noticed, amongst others— and set them down helter-skelter upon the table, putting knives and forks, one here and one there, for no reason in particular.

"What the food we ate was I have not a notion. There was a piece of fish, some vegetables, and once I found myself eating something that tasted like porridge. My thoughts, as you will conceive, were entirely absorbed in my neighbour. That sudden expression of grief, almost of panic, which had swept over her face was terrible to see, yet the look of repression, and patient endurance which presently replaced it, was almost worse. Although wholly innocent, of course, of having had any share in producing her troubles, I felt for the moment as if I had been guilty of them all. My sensations were dreadful. How was I, I asked myself, to break through this odious knot of circumstances in which I found myself bound? Other questions too poured across my mind. How did she come to be stranded there? the last survivor apparently of an entire family? Did those empty chairs really represent that father and those sisters of whom she had spoken, and was it possible that they were *all* dead? Had this hideous famine swept them all away, as it had swept away hundreds of thousands of humbler victims?

"Glancing at her from time to time across the table, I was struck with the strangely fixed expression of those wonderful eyes of hers. It was a look that haunted me; which has haunted me ever since. Could there be anything in it— not indeed of insanity, that I did not believe for a moment—but of imperfect comprehension, a partial paralysis of the mind, and was that the explanation of her curiously passive demeanour, as well as of the behaviour of the two old

servants ?   Her eyes were so widely open that
in any eyes less perfect one would have called
it staring.   It seemed to me as if everything
about us—the big dreary room ; the naked
wilderness of table-cloth ; the grey pool in the
gravel outside—all were reflected in their depths.
It was a terrible look to see, especially on the
face of one so young.   It was as though so
much that was heartrending and confusing had
passed before her eyes that they could never
become natural again ; could never lose that
expression of vacant misery ; could never cease
to see something—I did not know what—that
haunted them.

"You must forgive me," my old gentleman
here interrupted himself to say, " if I dwell too
long upon this part of my narrative, but the
fact is, I suppose I find a dismal pleasure in
doing so, and that it is the temptation of
talking it all over again after the lapse of so
many years that has led me into the egotism
of telling you my story at all.   Those eyes of
Eleanor d'Arcy have never quite passed out of
my life ; I can see them to-day, just as clearly
as I saw them forty-seven years ago.   You
smile—you think the explanation an easy one.
I fell in love with her, you say, and hence this
vividness of recollection.   In a sense you are

right. I *did* fall in love with her, though I don't think I fell in love with her then, at that first moment. In short, I will own that it was largely stimulated by the fact of finding that there was a rival before me in the field, a fact of which I was not left in ignorance longer than the very next morning.

" I was up early, and had been going over the instructions drawn out for my guidance, none of which included any hint as to how I was to deal with the family of the late unfortunate proprietor. I was standing before the fire, pondering rather gloomily over the matter, when the old woman, whose name I had found to be Nora O'Connor, opened the door, with an air of stealth peculiar to herself, paddled across the floor, and, coming close up to me, informed me in a whisper that his honour Mr. Henry O'Hara was beyont, and would I spake wid him for a minute?

"'And who the——' I began; then checked myself. 'Who is Mr. Henry O'Hara?' I asked impatiently.

"'Auch, doesn't yer 'anner know who Mr. Henry O'Hara is? O my God!'

" The idea of such ignorance seemed to paralyze her remaining faculties, for she stood still, gasping and staring.

" ' No, I don't,' I answered.   ' However, show him in, whoever he is.'

" The order was unnecessary, for, getting tired, I suppose, of waiting in the porch until his envoy returned, the visitor at this moment tapped at the door, and, without waiting for an answer, walked in.

" He was a very tall young man of about my own age, immensely broad in the chest, yet with an air of great activity. Perhaps the most striking feature at first sight was the excessive redness of his hair, which, as he took off his hat at the door, literally seemed to blaze, and which rose in a fiery crest at the top of his head. Red-haired men are, in my experience, usually ugly ones, but this man was certainly an exception to that rule. His complexion was clear, and he wore, what was still somewhat unusual, a moustache, one which was several degrees darker than his hair. His eyes were light, blue or grey, I am not sure which, but large, and capable, as I soon found, of emitting a sufficiently fierce light when their owner chose. He was dressed in a cut-away coat, with ill-made top boots, and carried a large riding-whip with a gilt knob in his hand. Take him altogether, he was a remarkably good-looking young man, but he was not

—or so I rapidly decided—what is commonly known as a gentleman.

"'Good-morning to you, sòr. I took the liberty of stepping within, me good friend there being sometimes a little tedious in her movements,' he began, with a strong, but not disagreeable brogue, scanning me at the same time with what I felt to be a decidedly scrutinizing glance.

"'My little place—that is to say, me brother's little place—is only three miles off up the hill yonder, so I call most days to inquire after Miss Eleanor d'Arcy. I am sorry to hear from old Nora that——'

"He stopped suddenly, and again looked at me with the same scrutinizing expression as before, one which I instinctively found myself resenting.

"'I have not had the pleasure of seeing Miss d'Arcy this morning,' I said very stiffly. An antagonism against this man, a latent rivalry, had begun to rise in my breast almost before he had opened his mouth.

"Whether the feeling was reciprocated on his part, or whether there was anything supercilious in my tone which annoyed him, I cannot say, but a fighting look came into his face, one which seemed to be carried right up to his crest of fiery-coloured hair. Irishmen are often accused of beating about the bush, but I am bound to say that this particular Irishman lost no time in coming to the point.

"'Then, I think, this being the beginning of our acquaintance, 'tis as well, sor, you should know——' Here he fixed his eyes upon me with an expression which, if not exactly menacing, was evidently prepared to become so at a moment's notice. 'As well you should know that I come here as a suitor'—he pronounced the word as if there were several *h*'s in it— 'a suitor for that young lady's hand.'

"I jumped up from my chair, and stood staring at him in astonishment from the hearthrug.

"'Yes, sor, as a suitor,' he repeated, aspirating the word this time as if there were at least six *h*'s in it.

"Whether he felt that the announcement required some additional self-assertion, or whether from the beginning he had intended to assume a bellicose attitude, I do not know, but he squared his shoulders till they looked twice as broad as before, threw up his chin in the air, drew in his breath audibly, and stood staring at me across the room. 'That is my intention, sor! My intention is to *marry* Miss Eleanor d'Arcy, and I'd as lief you and every one else knew it,' he repeated.

"I stood staring at him. I had no right, of course, to object; I had nothing to say to the matter, yet I felt perfectly furious, and outraged, at the bare suggestion. Marry her !—this big, underbred, red-headed squireen! this local Apollo in a cut-away coat !—marry that lovely creature! that vision of delicacy and refinement ! It was no business of mine, of course, but I then and there mentally damned his impudence.

"The announcement seemed to relieve my visitor of any momentary awkwardness which the situation might have inspired, for it was in a comparatively placable and conversational tone that he next began to speak.

" 'That being the case you'll easily see, me dear sor—putting yourself I mean in my place —you'll easily see that the sooner the matter's settled and over the better. Is it fit—I ask you as a gentleman—is it fit that a lady like her—a d'Arcy of Castle d'Arcy, the finest blood in the county Galway, or any other—should stop on in this house, and it sold over her head to black strangers out of England? Is it fit that she—a lady bred and born if ever there was one—should be affronted by such a state of things as that?'

"By this time I had begun to realize that my first sensations were slightly irrational, consider-

ing that I had never seen or heard of Miss Eleanor
d'Arcy till the preceding evening. I detested
the man cordially, and would gladly have kicked
him down-stairs, had that been possible. As I
evidently could not do so however, at any rate
at present, I felt that I had better meet his very
undesired confidence in the spirit of a reasonable
ma n.

"'Really, sir,' I said, 'you make me feel
very awkward. I hardly know what I am to
say to all this. I am naturally flattered by
your confidence, but believe it was as unnecessary, as it was unlooked for. If you and Miss
d'Arcy'—the words seemed to stick in my
throat and I had the greatest difficulty in finish-
ing my sentence civilly—'If you and Miss
d'Arcy have made up your minds, what more
can there be to be said? In any case her
own relations are clearly the only persons who
can with the smallest propriety approach the
subject.'

"My visitor continued to stare at me for
some minutes after I had done speaking with an
air of perplexity.

"''Tis clear you don't understand the matter
at all, sor,' he said at last. 'Relations! God
help her, she hasn't one, nor the half of one
left. Not a soul has she on the face of the

earth to look after her this blessed minute but me, unless maybe 'tis yourself.'

"'Myself!' I exclaimed in a tone of astonishment, though I must own that my heart gave a sudden throb at the words. 'What right can I have to presume to interfere with Miss d'Arcy or her affairs? I am here by the purest accident, on a merely business errand, connected with the sale of the property. My stay will be of the shortest possible duration. In all probability I shall leave to-morrow, or next day at furthest.'

"'Thank God for that, any way!' cried my new acquaintance heartily. 'You'll excuse me, sor,' he added quickly. 'No incivility meant or intended, no more than if you were the man in the moon. Only it will be plain to you, as it would to any gentleman, that it is not what a gentleman could be expected to put up with, seeing another man, and a well-looking, personable young man—I'm only saying what that glass behind you can tell you—settled in the very house with her. And she but a child, as one may say, and an innocent one at that—ready to be led or guided by any one. I'm the last man to threaten a gentleman, not being in the laaste a quarrelsome man, but'—here he confronted me with an unmistakably combative light in his eyes—' 'tis a thing I couldn't put up with, so you may as well know it t'once.'

"'Confound you, sir!' I began. Then feeling the absurdity of quarrelling with such a man, and upon such a subject, I swallowed down my rage, and took refuge in an excess of formality. 'You do me far too much honour by supposing that my being here could have the smallest effect upon your interests,' I said stiffly. 'As I remarked before I have come here upon a strictly business errand. Miss d'Arcy was good enough to ask me to dine with her last night, but beyond that I have little hope or expectation of seeing anything of her. Moreover, were the case different,' this I added with a touch of spitefulness—'I hope I should have too much sense of honour to take advantage of the position of an unfortunate young lady, who, by some extraordinary hazard of fortune, has apparently been left utterly alone and unprotected in the world.'

"This was such a very direct, as well as a very uncalled-for, attack upon my part that I fully expected my irascible acquaintance to proceed at once to extremities. But it seems to be difficult in Ireland to predict when a man will or will not consider himself insulted, and so far from producing a pistol out of his pocket, my curious visitor looked suddenly quite crestfallen, and even conscience-stricken.

"'I declare to God, sir, I'm the last man to wish to do such a thing! the very last!' he said gloomily. ''Tisn't that I care about her relations either, if she had them itself, mind you; not if every d'Arcy in the county Galway was crammed together, and sitting in that arm-chair. But when I think of her wanting what she's accustomed to! I tell you if it was suffering any discomfort on my account I saw her, it would be blowing my brains out on the spot I would, no question of it!'

"There was so much genuine earnestness in the man's voice and manner, that in spite of my incipient rivalry, I could not help a certain feeling of pity, and even of sympathy for him, beginning to arise in my mind. 'Do you mean,' I said—'excuse the apparent impertinence of the question—but do I understand you to mean that you have no income of your own to support her with?'

"'Faith, not a single penny in the wide world,' he exclaimed frankly. 'You see the way of it is this. The little bit of money which came to me when me poor father died seven years back—well for him that he *did* die, seeing what was coming!—why I left it in the property, as a gentleman would. There wasn't one of us did otherwise, barring me eldest sister, that married a man out of Armagh—a nigger [1] he is, if ever there was one, though a clever lawyer. As for the rest of us, we left the bit of money in it, and I needn't tell you where it is now, with the rates close on twenty shillings in the pound, and me eldest brother himself with only his wife's money between him and the workhouse.'

" ' You have a profession ? ' I suggested mildly.

" ' Then indeed I have not,' he replied indignantly, and this time as though I had really offered him some deadly insult. ' What profession do you suppose me father's son would be likely to have, unless it was soldiering, and that's against me principles ? '

" I felt too dumfounded at first by this observation to attempt any reply. When I did so it was with the feeling that I had got into a labyrinth, out of which I possessed no clue. ' Do you mean that you object to soldiering in the abstract ? ' I inquired helplessly.

" At that he laughed, a great jovial laugh that rang through the empty room like a trumpet.

" ' Bless me, sor, do I look like a man that would object to soldiering in the abshtract ? '

[1] Niggard ; niggardly fellow.

he cried. And to do him justice he certainly did not.

"'By me principles, I mean that I'm not—not altogether exactly right with the Government at present, don't you see. If I wasn't out with those that got into trouble the other day, it was by accident so to speak, and owing to the want of time. The whole thing was got up in such a devil of a hurry. 'Twas over, you may say, before 'twas rightly begun. I'd have been out with them fast enough if they'd have given me the chance, but before I knew they meant fighting, all the fighting there was was over. A poor business they made of it; a desperate poor business from find to finish!'

"This promised to be rather interesting, but since Mr. O'Hara's affairs were really no concern of mine, I felt that I had received enough of his confidences for the present. Accordingly I made an excuse, and left him for the moment in possession of the field.

II

"My business that morning was to see as much as I could of the property, and to make up my mind about it as soon as possible. Accordingly,

though a fine rain was falling, and the sky so
lowering that it seemed to be only a few yards
above my head, I donned a mackintosh, pulled
a pair of leggings over my boots, and was soon
trudging down the carriage drive, and into the
region beyond.

"I had almost forgotten the look of stony
desolation which had so impressed me the
previous evening.   As I passed out through
the gate, it suddenly burst upon me again, and
I had not gone many hundred yards before I
found myself knee-deep, so to speak, in stones,
stones of every size and shape, but all of a
blackish-grey colour, and under them the scanty
herbage seemed to be suffocated.

"The impression which the whole scene con-
veyed was as if some tremendous hailstorm, with
rocks instead of hailstones, had recently occurred.
For every blade of grass there seemed to be five
stones, for every patch of potatoes or oats, there
must have been a thousand.

"How, even under the most favourable circumstances, a population of any size could have
found the means of subsistence, I was at a loss
to guess, yet, from the number of empty cabins
on every side, it had evidently been thickly
populated, and not long before either.

"It seemed a mockery that the only work

o

which the remaining inhabitants appeared to find
to do was the occupation of stone-breaking.   I
passed a dozen men at one place, sitting by the
roadside, each armed with a hammer, which
he was listlessly bringing down upon the stones
as I passed.   These, and a group of women and
children huddled for shelter behind a wall, were
literally the only human beings I saw all the
time I was out.

" Tired with walking over the stones, sick
at heart at the misery of everything I witnessed, and fully resolved to have nothing to
say to such an investment, I went back about
three o'clock to the house, and roamed idly
round it for some time without meeting any
one.   It was a roomy old structure, ugly rather
than otherwise, but with a certain stamp of
dignity and hospitality about it, which even its
present dismantled condition could not entirely
efface.   I caught glimpses through the windows
of a couple of drawing-rooms, and there seemed
to be other sitting-rooms beyond.   Leaving the
front of the house, I passed through a shrubbery,
up a short path between tall evergreens, and
into a stable-yard, which lay at the back of the
house.   It was empty, and almost completely
grass-grown ;   most of the stable-doors were
shut, but one happened to be open as I passed,

and, looking in, I saw five or six loose boxes, and a number of stalls, all in fairly good order, but all untenanted, with the exception of a small donkey, which showed its innocent grey muzzle below a rack meant evidently for more dignified animals.

"I had made the circuit of the yard, and was on the point of leaving it, when I came to a wall, with a large door opening in the centre of it. This door being open, I passed through, and found myself in an inner yard. It was deserted, like the first, but not yet grass-grown, and in the middle of it stood a couple of huge copper caldrons, capable of containing perhaps fifty gallons apiece, with a primitive cooking arrangement under each, and a long bench or table, with stools at intervals. It was not at these things, however, that my gaze was riveted, but upon a slight figure in black, sitting motionless upon a stool in the middle of this scene of desolation. It was Eleanor d'Arcy. Evidently she had not heard my approach, for she continued to sit upon her stool, her eyes bent upon the ground, her hands hanging listlessly before her, her whole attitude one of absorbed and concentrated melancholy.

"I stood still for a minute, not venturing

to approach her, but was about to give some
signs of my presence, when she suddenly flung
her arms down upon the table before her,
and, hiding her face in them, burst out crying, or rather wailing, with a long-drawn
moan of anguish that rings through my memory
still.

"The old woman, Nora O'Connor, who must
have been hovering somewhere near at hand,
ran into the yard the instant she heard that
cry, and squatting down on the ground beside
her mistress, put one arm about her, and with
the other began gently patting her on the
back, uttering at the same time the sort of
crooning sounds which nurses often do to comfort some child that has hurt itself. But the
poor girl only turned away from her with a
louder moan of desolation.

"'Oh, Ann, Ann! Where are you? Sister
dear, *do* come to me!' she cried.

"Getting up from her stool, she looked all
round; at the empty yard; at the benches, and
the table, and the caldrons; looked at it all as
if somewhere the person whom she sought *must*
be found; the tears meanwhile streaming down
her face, her hands locked together, and her
whole expression that of a child given over to
the most complete despair. Suddenly she caught

sight of me, standing in the open doorway. She
did not however avert her gaze, as might have
been expected. On the contrary she looked at
me with exactly the same appealing expression, as if to ask if *I* could not help her, if
I could not somehow find her sister for her?
Then after a minute she turned, and, followed
by the old woman, went out of the yard, and
back into the house.

"I, too, presently left the yard, and wandered
away, I knew not where, stirred to the very
depths of my soul, by that look of appeal;
feeling as if it were tugging at my very heart-
strings. I got upon the grass, and struck across
it to the shore, where I wandered about for
hours, heedless of where I was going, thinking
only of her. I passed below the old black
tower upon the point, and up again to where
the shore rose steeply, and I could see across the
stone-encumbered country, to a line of cloud-
covered mountains which stretched towards the
north. I looked at all this, but I saw nothing
clearly. I saw only Eleanor d'Arcy's face, with
those great tear-filled eyes turned in appeal upon
myself. My love for her sprang up full-grown
in that instant. I loved her, I told myself so, I
swore that I would win her. I never stopped
to consider the hindrances; never asked myself

how far it was possible. I was in love, and for the first time in my life.

"It seems strange to remember the follies one commits under such circumstances," my old gentleman went on after a pause. " I remember striding about that afternoon, and feeling as if I owned everything I could see; feeling as if she and I were going to be king and queen of this wide domain which her ancestors had once possessed. The weather got worse and worse; the wind rose and whistled amongst the stones; rags of seaweed blew against my face like dead leaves, but I walked about as if on air. As for the dreariness it was no longer dreary to me. It excited me; made me feel as if I were some sort of a hero. I remember shouting at the top of my voice, and leaping as I raced along the shore, so that any one who had happened to see me that afternoon would have thought that I had gone stark mad. My love was like a bonfire on a winter's night, and everything seemed to be as fuel to its heat. Even what I couldn't help knowing to be the disadvantages of the situation; her helplessness; the sort of collapse which had evidently over-taken her mind, all this made me only love her the more. I told myself that I would marry her; that I would take her away from this

dreary place, with all its dreadful memories ;
that she should find warmth, love, and comfort elsewhere ; that she would forget her old
troubles ; would take new root in a new place;
that everything in short would be different, and
that everything would end rightly.

" Well, I may pass over all my raptures,
which are neither very interesting, nor, I suppose, particularly original, seeing that every
man has gone through much the same experience, and will go on to tell you the end of this
Galway adventure of mine. I remained at
Castle d'Arcy for several weeks longer. I could
have left sooner, of course, but did not choose
to do so, and therefore told myself that it was
my business to stay. I saw a great deal of
Eleanor d'Arcy during that time. We used to
eat our meals together, and sometimes she would
linger a little while in the dining-room after
they were finished, and now and then I was
able to persuade her to walk with me as far as
the little summer-house upon the shore, where
she would sit for an hour or more, looking,
in the passive, helpless fashion peculiar to her,
at the sea. She even grew to be rather
attached to me, I think, in a placid, clinging sort
of way. I talked to her, of course, about my
devotion, and no doubt poured out a hundred

absurdities at her feet. She, in her turn, talked
to me, but never in reply to what I said ;
always about her sisters ; about their life together; and generally as if they were still alive ;
though sometimes in the middle of a sentence
she would stop short, and begin to look around
her, with that peculiarly wistful expression of
hers, which always went straight to my heart.

" Mr. O'Hara came a good deal to Castle
d'Arcy during this time, and to him also she
would talk in much the same gentle, dreamy
fashion as she did to me ; stopping often in the
middle of something she was saying, as if listening for a step on the stairs, or a voice in the
hall ; for those footsteps and those voices which
she would never hear again. We could neither
of us say that she encouraged us, and yet in
a sense she did, for she was always, not only
gentle, but even grateful, as if pleased by
every kind word, and only longing for more.
I believed, and still believe, that she would
have accepted either of us, not me more than
him, or him than me, but whichever of us
had pressed our claims the first, and the most
vigorously upon her attention. She seemed
to be helplessly looking for some support ;
to be pining and sickening for it. She was
utterly incapable of thinking or planning out

any course of action for herself, while, on the other hand, she was evidently perfectly willing to fall into any plan that some one else chose to lay out for her.

"Looking back at the whole circumstance, it seems inconceivable that she should have had no one to stand by her in such a juncture of her life except two young men, neither of whom were any relation to her, and neither of whom could certainly have been called disinterested. Whether the extreme isolation of the property had cut her off from the rest of the world, whether every one was so occupied with his own affairs as to be indifferent to others, or whether again it really was not known that one of the d'Arcy family was still living in the old home, certain it is that not a soul seemed to heed what became of her. No one came near the house all the time I was there; no one wrote, or took any trouble about her. The only other house of any size within miles of Castle d'Arcy was the O'Haras', and its solitary inhabitant was at present young Mr. Henry O'Hara himself. His elder brother had been a tenant, I found, of Mr. d'Arcy, and had acted for some years as his agent, but had now left the country. He was said to have been a very bad agent and his management to have contributed not a little to the collapse that had befallen the property, but in all probability this was merely a question of time, and if ruin had not come when it did, it must have followed soon afterwards.

"Anyhow there she was, absolutely alone, and that some decision about her future must be come to was clear. And there were we two young men, and the matter had to be fought out single-handed between us. Every time Mr. O'Hara and myself met, we glared more and more ferociously at one another. There was no pretence on my part now of not being his rival. I hated him cordially, and probably he hated me, if anything, rather worse. To get an extra look from her, or an extra chance of walking, or sitting beside her, we would either of us have cut the other's throat with the greatest pleasure in life.

"The two old servants of the house kept the balance pretty evenly between us, one of them inclining to O'Hara's side, and the other to mine. Oddly enough it was the old man, who had at first been so furiously opposed to me, who came round to my side, while the old woman, though obsequiously civil, would have nothing to say to me, but sidled away whenever I tried to approach her. I will

not deny that poor O'Connor's new-found
regard for me was due in the first instance to
certain objects which—Heaven forgive me—I
produced out of my pocket for his benefit,
but I think that it also sprang from a deep-
seated dislike and contempt which he evidently
felt for the O'Hara family, as well as from the
satisfaction of having some new auditor to
whom he could discourse upon the past greatness,
glory, and grandeur of the d'Arcy family.

"He would come stealing out of the house to
join me of a morning as I stood looking across
the sea, or strolled to and fro over the cushions
of thyme and pink thrift which covered the
upper rocks.   Below this point began that long
black reef of rocks, which I mentioned before,
and which was almost like a natural pier, running far out into the sea, and joined to the
shore artificially by a flight of rough stone steps,
mounting up to the little summer-house which
surmounted the top of the point.

"'Miss Ann's thrack'—that was what old
O'Connor called this natural pier, and he would
tell me wonderful tales about Miss Ann, and
about the dance she used to lead her suitors,
who from his account numbered every unmarried
man in the county, all at least that could have
ventured to aspire to a d'Arcy of Castle d'Arcy.

" ' 'Twasn't her *looks*, no, 'twasn't Miss Ann's
looks,' he would say, shaking his old white
head with an air of mystery—'though she
was a fine-looking lady, too ; big in the body,
like all the d'Arcys, and a fine colour in her
cheeks, and the clearest skin in the country.
No, no, 'twasn't her looks, 'twas her *ways*.
She had ways of her own that was like no one
else's that ever was born, and no man ever
come nigh her that could stand out against
them ! Why, yer honour, she'd talk to them
about ghosts, maybe, or marmaids, or say-
divils, or the like of that, till she'd terrify
their very souls out of their bodies, and then
she'd soothe and soother them down again, so
that you'd think 'twas their own mother she
was, no less ! And the fun of her ! I've
heard her talking in that little tay-house up
there, and she pouring out the tay at the time,
and there would be six or seven of them
courtin' her 'tonce ; just hanging on the lips
of her, and beggin' and prayin' of her to
marry them. Young Mr. Blakeney of Castle
Blakeney, and Mr. Pearse, and the old Lord's
son from near Athenry, and Major O'Keefe,
and the rest of the officer-gentlemen quartered
at Galway—not that she'd ever have looked
at one of *thim*. And talk ! I tell you she

could talk the birds off the trees, or the fishes out of the say pools, so she could! And laugh! She'd just make you drop off your seat with laughing, and with the quick turns of her! Her tongue was like her feet, and they were the two nimblest feet in the whole county of Galway.

"'"Marry you indade!" she'd say, when they would be pressing of her. "I'll jist tell you what I'll do. I'll marry any one of you that catches me up on me own thrack, before I gets to the end of it, and that's more than any of you will do!" Those would be Miss Ann's own words, and with that she'd lep up from her seat in the tay-house, and away with her down them steps like so much lightning. 'Twasn't the goats of Aranmore opposite that could teach her to run, nor yet to lep either, so they couldn't,—Miss Ann! To see her tearing down them steep stairs, and along that thrack, and the say, as yer honour can see, only a little way from her feet, and deep enough, God knows, to drown any one! And the gentlemen they would be after her, trying to catch her up; and fighting, and scrambling, and pulling at one another, seeing who'd get first! Slippin' too on the rocks, they'd be, and sliding over the sayweed, and

the Major's spurs catching in the cracks, and
Mr. Blakeney—that always was a hard swearer
—cursing so you'd think the very birds would
be frighted to hear him !   Oh, glory, glory,
but 'twas a wonderful sight.   As for catching
her, it would be out on that bit of far rock
you see there, in the middle of the say, standing on it, and waving her bit of handkercher
at them, she'd be, almost before they'd started.
Miss Elly she'd sit in the tay-house, and
laugh, fit to split.   It was the only times I
ever seen Miss Elly laugh, for she was always
a peaceable, quite creature, not like Miss Ann,
that was all spirit and life, like the wind.
A curious thing 'twas to look at them, and
think they were sisters at all, and they so
different.

"' Fond of one another ?   Fond is no name
for it, sor !   My God, they *were* fond of one
another.   Miss Elly she'd sit and look at Miss
Ann by the hour, and anything that belonged
to Miss Ann, if it was only an old pair of
gloves, she'd hold it, and kiss it, just the same
as if it was herself.   She was Miss Ann's
shadder, just her shadder.   Why the mother
of the two of them died when Miss Elly was
born, and Miss Ann was Miss Elly's mother,
and no better mother she needed either, though

it was but a shlip of a young lady she was
herself at the time ; just a shlip, Miss Ann !

" ' Miss Elly the handsomest, sor ? Why
Lord bless your honour, no man in the county
of Galway ever so much as *looked* at Miss Elly,
nor *thought* of her, when Miss Ann was in
it ! She was just her shadder, as I tell you.
And to think that there's nothin' now only the
shadder left ! Oh, my God, my God ! '

" I used to try to extract old O'Connor's
real opinion of my rival, and would now and
then bring the conversation dexterously round
to the subject of the O'Hara family, but the
old fellow was very cautious, and it was not
easy to draw him out upon that subject.

" ' Dacent people ; yes indade, very dacent,
couldn't be more so,' he would say. There
were some high O'Haras in the county, but
he had never seen any of them himself. As
for Mr. O'Hara he was 'a fine-grown young
man, a very fine-grown young man,' and that
was about all he could be induced to say
about him.

" From the peculiar screw which he gave
to his mouth when he spoke of them it was
easy, however, to see that he regarded the inferior family as simply so much dirt under
the feet of his own masters, and that the bare

notion of one of them aspiring to lift his eyes
to a d'Arcy was almost too audacious to have
come within his idea of what was possible.
At the same time I have no reason to flatter
myself that he regarded me as in any degree
worthier, indeed, for all I could tell to the
contrary, rather less so.

"Well, I must pass on, or I shall be all
night over my story. You can easily imagine
how O'Hara and I hated one another, and how
my hopes and fears rose or fell, according as
he or I seemed to be getting the advantage,
and I will go on now to tell you how this
rivalry of ours came to an end, and what finally
settled the matter, though *why* it should have
settled it, is more than I have ever been able
to explain satisfactorily to myself.

"I had gone one afternoon with Miss d'Arcy
to the 'tay-house,' as old O'Connor called it,
and we had been sitting together for some time
in the doorway, looking out over the sea. The
weather was rather wild, and finding that she
had brought no cloak or other wrap with her,
I offered to go back to the house and look
for one, leaving her sitting by herself in the
doorway.

"I had been to the house, and had got back
to the point of the slope from which the little

summer-house became visible, when, looking
towards it, I saw, to my surprise, that Miss
d'Arcy was no longer there. In another
moment I saw where she was. She had gone
down the steep, rocky steps, and was at that
moment walking slowly along the narrow track
—'Miss Ann's thrack'—and looking from
side to side, as if seeking for something or
some one that she expected to find there.

" Now that particular reef of rocks had always
seemed to me to be a remarkably dangerous place
to walk on, even in calm weather, and just then
there was a good deal of breeze, and the waves
were breaking every minute across the portion
which ran furthest out to sea, leaving a gap
between it and the big rock in which it
ended.

" I was so terrified at seeing her there that I
could hardly stir, and, though I tried to hurry,
I was aware that I made remarkably slow progress. Miss d'Arcy meanwhile walked quietly
along till she came to the gap near the end.
There she stopped, and stood looking down at
the space of water, which was at one moment
quite wide, while at the next it would shrink
till it seemed to be a mere thread of silver.
Here she waited a little while ; then suddenly
tried to spring across the water, as, from old

P

O'Connor's account, her sister Miss Ann was in the habit of doing.

"Whether her foot slipped, or whether the space itself was too wide, or what happened I do not know, but in any case she fell, and lay there, with the water washing right across her; evidently utterly unable to recover herself, and certain, as it seemed to me, to be washed into the sea by the next big wave.

"I ran for my life, as you may imagine. Never shall I forget the horrible sensation of seeing her there; seeing the waves go right across her, and being unable to get at her; feeling certain every moment that I should see her washed away before my eyes. By this time she was clinging with both hands to the seaweeds, but they were evidently giving way, and could hardly be expected to last more than another minute or two. My heart was in my mouth, my legs seemed to be made of lead, and I felt, rather than saw, that I should be too late. Those horrible green rollers kept curling over her, and the great brown strands of oarweed circling in the water under her feet. It was like a nightmare, and, just as in a nightmare, my legs seemed to be tied together, and my knees to knock, so that I could hardly move. I had got to where the rocks began, but had still a considerable distance to go, when I heard a shout a little to the left of me, and the next minute there came a sound of thundering footsteps, the footsteps of some one tearing down the steep slope, which at this point broke almost sheer into the sea. I looked in the direction, and saw—with a curious mixture of relief and fury—that some one was before me. It was O'Hara, of course. How he had contrived to appear upon the scene so exactly in the nick of time, I do not know, but in one moment from the time I heard his first shout, he seemed to be down the slope; to have crossed the steep piece at the bottom, which was below the reef; to have jumped into the sea; to have swum to the reef, and clambered to the top of it; to have got hold of Miss d'Arcy; picked her up in his arms, and to be marching back with her to the house.

"He came close to where I was standing, mad with rage, and hardly able to keep myself from rushing upon him, and dragging, or trying to drag her away. He took no notice of me, however, neither did she; indeed she lay like a baby in his arms, with her eyes shut, and her face dead white. He walked straight on to the house, and up the stairs, with the air of a man who has a right to do so. I followed them slowly, but, having reached the door, I remained outside upon the grass, with the jealousy and hatred of ten thousand fiends tearing and gnawing at my breast.

"Five minutes later he came out again, wearing a look of open triumph upon his face, and walked straight up to where I was standing.

"As I have already told you, he was an extremely well-built, handsome man, and on this occasion he looked handsomer than I had ever seen him look before. The wetness of his clothes, which brought out the splendid muscles of his arms and back, made him look also several degrees bigger than usual.

"'*Well, sor!*' he said. So far as I can remember that was all that he did say, but the tone was enough. I could feel that he was simply swelling all over with triumph; that he looked upon the rivalry between himself and me as ended; that he considered that he had won her; and that there was nothing further for me to say or to do in the matter.

"I scowled at him furiously, but I also accepted my defeat, though, as I said before, I never could explain to myself why I did so.

"'All right,' I said sullenly, answering the tone rather than the words. 'Don't let her *starve*, if you can help it; that's all!' And

I turned on my heel, and went off down the walk.

"It was an extremely mean thing for me to have said, seeing that he could not possibly help his own poverty, and why I said it I cannot understand, any more than I can understand why I should have felt that the mere fact of his having saved her life, while I had failed to do so, should have decided the matter between us. I can only suppose that there are occasions, even in these days, when a struggle of the sort between two men tends to reduce itself to a question of thews and sinews, and that the best man, physically speaking, wins. It was almost as if we had been running a race, as old Connor declared the suitors of 'Miss Ann' used to do, and that O'Hara, having won it, had in consequence secured the prize.

"Possibly—for I don't want to make myself out any better than I was—I may have had a feeling at the back of my mind that to bring home this poor, beautiful, distracted creature as my bride would have been a terribly rash proceeding. Men are cautious animals at bottom, even when they are most in love, and that may have had something to say to the odd submissiveness, not even yet accountable to myself, with which I yielded up the prize for which we had both been struggling.

"After this there was nothing further for me to do. I simply stood aside, and let matters take their course, as they would have done if I had never appeared upon the scene at all. Fearful, I suppose, of any further delay, O'Hara took the whole business into his own hands, and the arrangements for their marriage were carried out by him with the utmost rapidity. As for Elly herself, she, poor dear, was like a child in his hands. I believed then, and have always believed, that had I taken her destiny into mine, and asked her to come away with me, she would have agreed to do so. As matters stood, it was O'Hara who had asked her to go with him, and their destination was to be America.

"It came to the last day. I had kept out of the way as much as I could, though an obstinate determination to see the end of it had prevented my leaving Castle d'Arcy till all was over. It was settled that they were to be married in Galway, where O'Hara had some relations, and next day they were to sail in an emigrant ship for New York. Old Nora was to accompany her young mistress, and her husband was to follow them, whenever sufficient money for his journey could be found.

" The evening before they left I went to say good-bye to Miss d'Arcy, and was coming out of the house when I suddenly ran up against O'Hara, almost exactly on the same spot where we had parted so angrily the day of her adventure upon the reef.

" He was passing on, without taking any notice of me, but I stopped him abruptly.

" 'Stop a moment please, Mr. O'Hara,' I said. 'Everything is over now. You have won her, and there is nothing more to be said. I spoke to you very uncivilly the other day, but you must acknowledge that you would probably have done the same, had my case been yours. What I want to say to you now is simply this—For God's sake be careful of her! And, look here——' I pulled a leaf out of a memorandum book, and held it towards him —'I want you to take this address, and to promise me that if ever you are in any difficulty; if ever she—if ever—if—if there is ever *anything* I can do for her, that you will let me know? Will you promise me this?'

" He looked at me for a moment between the eyes.

" 'I will, sor. Before God I will. You're a gentleman. Good-bye to you, sor,' he said.

" It *was* good-bye, for I never saw either of

them again. The next day they went off very early in the morning to Galway, and I returned to England."

My old gentleman was silent for a considerable time after he had finished his story, and I also said nothing. At last—"Did you never see her again?" I inquired.

"Never," he answered.

"And did Mr. O'Hara never write to you?"

"Never," he repeated. "From that day to this I have never been able to learn anything about either of them."

He was again silent, and I also sat still, partly from not wishing to disturb him, partly because his story had set me thinking of many things. The rest of our party had long since gone to bed, and the house was absolutely silent. Presently I got up, went over to a window, opened it, and looked out. A fragment of creeper, which had got loose, had kept flapping against the wall with a small, persistent, tapping noise during all the latter part of the story. The view from this window I was standing at, though nothing special to boast of in the matter of beauty, was rather a cheerful one in the day-time ; a road, running past the house to the nearest country town, being visible through a break in the trees, so that there was generally a glimpse of people coming and going, and a comfortable stir of wheels. At this hour, however, there was nothing, and, but for that tiny persistent tapping of the creeper, the silence would have been absolute. A small pond, which lay in a hollow below the house, shone with a dull cold gleam, which, on looking closer, I perceived to come from the reflection of a star twinkling immediately above it. It was September, and the air was already beginning to feel chilly. The branches of the trees kept rocking monotonously backwards and forwards, with a slow recurrent movement, and, through a break between two of them, I could distinguish a long stretch of empty road, which seemed to be stretching dully away to all infinity.

IRISH HISTORY CONSIDERED AS
A PASTIME

It is notoriously difficult to know what will
really appeal to our youngers and betters!
Unless administered very carefully, and in the
insinuating guise of a story, history in my
experience rarely does so, though why it does
not do so it is less easy to explain satisfactorily.
The obvious explanation probably is that so
long as people are extremely busy in concoct-
ing imaginary history for themselves, the history
that is already cut, dried, and laid upon a shelf,
is too thin, and too remote a business, for the
natural grossness of youthful egotism to relish.
This may be so, yet other pursuits seem able
to overcome that obstacle, so why not this
one? Looking back with as hearty a con-
centration of egotism as I can summon for the
occasion, I must confess that beyond a dim,
probably quite unwarrantable, predilection in

favour of the Black Prince, or of Highland
Charlie, I cannot remember caring greatly in
my early youth for the history of any country,
including the country to which I belonged, and
which I certainly, after my own feeble little
fashion, loved.

And by early youth I do not even mean the
obscure realm of babyhood, but that comparatively well-lit and well-explored country which
lies about us as we near our twelfth, thirteenth,
and fourteenth birthdays. Before that date the
distaste for history, as for most other pursuits
affected by our elders, goes without saying.
It is not alone then the history which exists
only upon dull, printed pages—pages in which
Greeks, Romans, and Frenchmen ; Nebuchad-
nezzar and Napoleon Buonaparte, all appear
to have lived about the same time, and to be
equally dull and unnecessary persons. It is also
the history which is still walking visibly about
the world—which, like Adam in the famous
German play, may almost be seen crossing the
stage on its way to be created—even this
description of history we are far too self-
respecting to take any notice of, or to lift up
our heads from our own concerns to consider.

And if the subject generally is thus rather at a
discount, it is hardly, I fear, to be expected that

Irish history would prove the one marked and favoured exception ! Even those whose palates have grown hardened by a course of the most arid literary provender have pronounced that particular form of diet to be exceedingly unpalatable. What hope, therefore, that it would find favour in a quarter where to be entertaining is your one chance of recognition? Possibly if it were discreetly whispered in this same quarter that the study is not one favourably looked upon as a rule by elders, that might produce a certain reaction in its favour. So far, however, no master-hand has undertaken to serve it up in such a manner as to give it even a hope of success with those particularly difficult critics. Indeed I must confess that, as a whole, I cannot imagine any one succeeding in doing so ; the bare thought of such a task being calculated to awaken terror in any moderately discerning mind.

In judiciously selected fragments, on the other hand, a good deal might, it seems to me, be done. Few historical personages, for instance, seem to have been more clearly laid out by nature to be a boy's hero than Gerald, or, as he was usually called by his contemporaries, Ger*oit* Mor, the eighth and greatest of all the Earls of Kildare. Everything he said and did, his whole standpoint and view of life, seem exactly modelled upon the standard of the third or fourth form. He was prepared, for instance, at any moment to fight his king ; he was even prepared, as will presently be seen, to set up a new king in place of the old one, when that old one had, in his opinion, misbehaved. Certain things, however, he would not do. He would not join hands with the common enemy, even when such joining would have been of advantage to him. He was the King's Irish Viceroy, and the King's Irish Viceroy, whatever happened, he was determined to live and die.

Personal prejudice in his favour apart, he really seems to have been a very delightful being, and his sayings and doings are full of the sense of a real, and a most vivid personality. As regards his outward man we are unfortunately rather in the dark, the art of the portrait painter never having greatly flourished in Ireland. No likeness of him, even the rudest, so far as I am aware, exists, nor have we even any piece of armour that he wore, or any weapon that he handled ; while of his chief house little remains save the naked walls, broken in his grandson's time by the cannon of Skeffington, and existing as a ruin to our own. Some meagre

personal descriptions there are, but how far they
correspond to the man as his contemporaries
knew him, must be guessed, less by evidence,
than by a process of imaginative reconstruction.
"A mightie man of stature," Holinshed tells
us he was, and as this is borne out by another
report, which describes him as "of tall stature
and good presence," we may safely regard it as
accurate. A big, broad-shouldered man, with a
good-natured, dominant face, somewhat heavy
about the region of the lower jaw. Though little
Celtic blood is traceable in his veins, there seems
to have been a considerable share of it in his
nature. "The Earl being soon hotte, and
soon colde, was well belooved," says the same
Holinshed. "He was open and playne, hardly
able to rule himself when moved ; in anger not
so sharp as short, being easily displeased, and
sooner appeased." A vehement, sharp-spoken
man, dangerous when opposed, but easily mollified
when once the occasion for anger was past ; a
man not difficult to move to laughter, and liking
a jest, even if it were sometimes at his own
expense. Thus anecdote tells that one day, he
"being at the tyme in hotte rage," one Maister
Boyce, "a gentleman retegned to him," was
offered a horse by another retainer on condition
that he would venture to "plucke an heare

(hair) from the earl hys bearde." Thereat, nothing daunted, Boyce, stepping up to the Earl, with whose good-nature he was probably thoroughly acquainted, said, "If it like your good lordshippe, one of your horsemen has promised me a choyce nagge if I do snippe one haire from your bearde." "Well," quoth the Earl, "I agree thereto, but if thou plucke out more than one, I promise to bring my fyst about thine eare."

Something like a leader this! Imagine the store of such anecdotes, of which this is but a sample, which must have been circulated round the camp fires, while the steaks were grilling, and the clothes drying, during those interminable expeditions which the Lord Deputy was forever waging against the O'Byrnes, the O'Tooles, the O'Connor Falys, or other of the "King's Irish enemies!" For Geroit Mor was essentially a fighter. He loved to be for ever in the saddle. He adored fighting for its own sake, and would have made a raid—so would most Irishmen of his day, or any other for that matter—were it to recover a strayed kid.

Everything we hear of him bears the same stamp. His talk smacks emphatically of the open air. He quickly sickened of courts and courtly places, even when not kept in them as a prisoner. His son's speech to Wolsey would have equally suited his own lips. " I slumber, my lord, in a hard cabyn, while your Grace sleeps in a bed of downe; I serve under the cope of Heaven, when you are served under a canapie; I drinke water out of my skull,[1] when you drinke wine out of golden cuppes; my courser is trayned to the field, when your genet is taught to amble. When you are begraced, crouched, and kneeled to, I find small grace with any of our Irish rebels, 'cept I myself cut them off by the two knees."

Wolsey, we are told, having all this suddenly fired at him, " rose up in a fume from the councayle table, perceiving Kildare to be no babe." Certainly none of the Kildares were babes; and their tongues were to the full as ready at an encounter as their swords. If the reader asks how far these utterances are or are not strictly historical, I confess that I am at a loss to reply. May one add that the matter is not of any profound consequence one way or other? Written down by contemporaries, they doubtless fitted well enough into the popular estimate of the men, or they would not have been told at all. Beyond this, who knows anything, with absolute certainty, about anybody?

---

[1] Skull-cap (?).

Let us be thankful if a few life-like fragments exist, and not scan their credentials too curiously. Certitude is not for this world, and certainly is not the peculiar prerogative of Ireland, or of Irish historians !

The most picturesque of the many exploits in which Geroit Mor figured so prominently was that famous Coronation scene which took place in Dublin in the year 1487, in the presence, not only of the Lord Deputy himself, but also of the Lord Chancellor, the Archbishop of Dublin, the Lord Birmingham of Athenry, the Lord Courcy of Kinsale, the Lord Nugent of Delvin, the Lord Plunket of Dunsany, and many other equally important personages.

It was not apparently until the last moment that it was discovered that no crown was forthcoming for this ceremony—Ireland having unfortunately for some time past possessed no sovereign of her own ! Accordingly one was hastily borrowed for the occasion from off the head of a statue of the Virgin " in St. Mary's Church by the Dame's Gate." Arrayed in this very celestial splendour the youthful monarch was mounted upon the shoulders of " Great Darcy of Plattin," celebrated as the tallest Irishman of his day, and so marched back to the castle, all his train following.

Who that youthful monarch really was seems hardly to be known even at this day. Whether, as King Henry's proclamation afterwards declared, he was " the son of Thomas Simnel, late of Oxford, joiner," seems never to have been decided to the absolute satisfaction of historians. In Ireland he was known at the time as Edward, Earl of Warwick, son of the Duke of Clarence, of Malmsey memory, who, having been born in Dublin, was naturally regarded with affection by its citizens. That there was another Earl of Warwick alive, and in King Henry's hands, was a matter which does not seem to have disturbed anybody's mind. This one was Dublin's own Warwick. This one had come to Ireland escorted by Martin Swart, that famous captain of mercenaries, and by two thousand German soldiers —tangible warriors of formidable appearance, and still more formidable appetites. Above all, this one was Geroit Mor's nominee, and therefore Earl of Warwick he was, and King he should be, if it rained Kings and Warwicks elsewhere for a week or more at a time.

So it was settled, and crowned accordingly he was. That ceremony over, however, Dublin began to feel the weight of its own spirited proceedings. To have a king of your own, no dim potentate hidden away in England, but a visible monarch, walking your own streets, and being saluted by your own citizens, was no doubt a very glorious possession. But to have to feed two thousand mercenaries—German ones !—in a country already eaten up with coyne, livery, and every species of exaction, was an infliction not long to be endured. Active operations accordingly were decided upon, no less active and simple than the conquest of England ! Kildare had to remain behind, seeing that Ireland would have got on badly in his absence, but it was decided that his brother, Sir Thomas Fitzgerald, should take command of such levies as could be got together, and that in company with all the late guests, he should get on shipboard, cross the channel, and prepare to take the field.

Off then went poor phantom King Simnel. Off went Simon the priest, who was his chief instructor in the part that he had to play. Off went Martin Swart, and his two thousand German mercenaries. Off went Lords Lovel and Lincoln, two English noblemen, who had come to Ireland to do homage to their new king. With them went also Sir Thomas Fitzgerald, who had resigned the office of Chancellor for the occasion. Landing at Foudray upon the 4th of June, they were joined by Sir Thomas

Broughton, and all marched triumphantly together towards Yorkshire.

They were met, however, by a crushing lack of enthusiasm. "Their snowball," in Lord Bacon's words, "did not gather as they went." Henry, by judicious clemency, had recently won popularity in the district. Scouts, stationed along the coast, sent tidings to him of all that was on foot. His army met Broughton and Swart with their followers close to the village of Stoke, about a mile from Newark-on-Trent. The fighting was severe, and lasted for three hours, but force was overwhelmingly on the side of the King. The Germans fought manfully ; the Irish levies "did right boldly, and stuck to it valiantly," but all was of no avail. The Earl of Lincoln was killed ; so also was Martin Swart, the leader of the German mercenaries ; so likewise was Sir Thomas Fitzgerald, and nearly the whole of the Irish contingent. Sir Thomas Broughton, while escaping from the battle-field, fell, it was said, into the Trent, and was drowned. Lord Lovel disappeared, and was never heard of again, tradition declaring that he had been dismally starved to death in a cellar in which he had hidden himself. Poor phantom King Simnel also disappeared, not into a cellar, but into a kitchen—the royal one—

whence he was destined to re-appear, very dis-
agreeably for his Irish supporters, in the days
to come.

Meantime in Dublin nothing was for a long
time heard of the fate of the expedition. In
what mood Geroit Mor waited for tidings
cannot be known, but may be sympathetically
guessed. At last they came. They could
scarcely have been blacker ! Ireland it seemed
was not to give a king to England. The whole
expedition had failed disastrously. Everything
was lost, and nearly every one concerned in it
was killed. The entire bubble, in short, had
burst, and as he pondered over the dismal
tidings Earl Gerald must have suspected that
the bursting of it could mean nothing less than
ruin to him and his.

That it ought to have meant ruin may fairly
be admitted. A few years later it certainly
would have meant it. Just then, however, affairs
were in such an extraordinarily complicated
condition that Henry soon found that it was
impossible for him to carry on the Government of Ireland except with the aid of the very
man who had just set up a new king in his
stead, and had actually dispatched an army to
England in the hope of overthrowing him !
Although another Deputy had been appointed,

it soon became evident that " our Rebel, the
Earl of Kildare," was the only person at once
strong enough and popular enough to hold that
very difficult and troublesome post ; while on
the other hand " our Rebel " himself was clearly
quite willing to wipe out the memory of his late
unfortunate *fiasco* as soon and as thoroughly as
might be.

Upon these terms of mutual interest a pact
accordingly was made. Henry agreed to pardon
the Earl, and even to continue him as his
Deputy. On the other side Kildare undertook
to sign a fresh oath of allegiance ; to abstain
from similar transgressions in the future ; and
to cross within twelve months to England,
there to make his submission in person.

The better to ratify this pact, the King determined to send as his Irish Commissioner the
comptroller of his household, Sir Richard Edgecombe, from whose diary we learn all that then
occurred.[1]   This part of the programme was
anything but acceptable, however, to the proud
taste of Geroit Mor.   To have to await the
Commissioner's arrival ; to receive him upon
the shore, and escort him respectfully through

[1] " The Voyage of Sir Richard Edgecombe, Kt., sent
by the King's Grace into Ireland."   Printed in Harris's
Hibernica, Dublin, 1747, p. 26.

the streets of Dublin—those streets which had recently witnessed such a very different pageant —was not a part in which he saw himself performing ! He did not hesitate for a moment. Sir Richard Edgecombe was to sail at the end of June, and early in July Geroit Mor announced his intention of starting for a pilgrimage to the shrine of the Miraculous Virgin of Trim. And thither three days later he departed, taking his usual bodyguard of some two hundred horsemen along with him.

Meanwhile Sir Richard had sailed from Cornwall in a ship called the *Anne of Fowey*, with a convoy of three smaller vessels, and five hundred soldiers as a guard. Touching first at Kinsale and Waterford—towns which, being in fierce opposition to the Deputy, received him with open arms—he proceeded to Dublin, encountering on his way " contraryous winds," so that only, he tells us, with " grate painn and perill " he succeeded at last in reaching Lambay Island, where his vessel cast anchor.

Here he was met by the news of the Viceroy's absence ! Absent, and at such a moment ? For what reason ? Upon a pious pilgrimage it was explained ; the Earl of Kildare, as all men knew, being a very religious nobleman. The days of pious pilgrimages were by no means yet over, so that Sir Richard had to put up with the excuse, and to digest his wrath as he best might. It soon appeared that there was very little else for him to digest, and this was an additional offence. To arrive spent, sore, weary, sea-sick, and to find this sort of greeting ! To be received with *this* sort of welcome ! Yet there are people who pretend that Ireland is a hospitable country !

Fortunately " the Ladye of Sir Peter Talbot," lord of Malahide, took pity upon the King's Commissioner, brought him to her own house, fed, and comforted him. Next day, Sir Richard rode to Dublin, where he was received by the mayor and principal citizens, who accompanied him to the Dominican Friary, where he was to take up his quarters during his temporary stay. As for the Earl of Kildare, he neither appeared, nor sent, nor gave the slightest indication of being aware that anything unusual was afoot !

Five days did Sir Richard Edgecombe remain nursing his wrath amongst the Dominicans— " to his gret costs and chargis," as he specially insisted that the King should be informed. Never since Royal Commissioners were invented had one been treated in so scurvy a fashion ! If he did not yearn to convert that Royal Pardon, of which he was the bearer, into a Royal Warrant for hanging and quartering, he must have been more than mortal. Fume as he might, there was nothing, moreover, to be done but to wait until the Deputy chose to come back. Despite of all that had occurred, Geroit Mor was still the King's representative in Ireland, and, if he insisted upon visiting shrines and saying his prayers till Christmas, Sir Richard must sit and devour his impatience as he best could amongst the Dominicans until he returned.

At last, upon July 12, Geroit Mor came riding quietly into Dublin, followed by his two hundred horsemen, and took up his abode at his residence of St. Thomas's Abbey, or, as it was then called, Thomas Court.

Here, as soon as he had shaken off the dust of his journey, he dispatched the Bishop of Meath, accompanied by Lord Slane, to summon the King's Commissioner into his presence. Upon his arrival at Thomas Court, Sir Richard was received in the "great chamber of the Abbey," Lord Nugent of Courcy, Lord Plunket, and other members of the Council—all enthusiastic supporters of the late King Simnel—being present. The King's Commissioner and the King's Deputy were at last face to face.

The meeting which followed these unusual

preliminaries was hardly to be called cordial. In his own report of the proceedings Sir Richard expressly informs us that he delivered the King's letter to the Earl "with no Reverencies or Courtesie," also that he made a short speech "not without Bitternesse." Bitterness indeed it would have been hard to grudge him under the circumstances, if he found it to be any comfort. Moreover, his troubles were by no means even yet over. No business was to be proceeded with upon that day. Certain of the Lords of the Council, he was told, were still absent, consequently everything must be deferred till they arrived. The next day was a Sunday, and Sir Richard and the Deputy attended mass together at Christ Church, the same church in which King Simnel had been crowned the year before, and, as on that occasion, the sermon was preached by "Payne, the lord Bushopp of Meathe," who was a devoted friend and adherent of the Earl of Kildare.

Monday, July 14, was the day fixed for the Deputy and the other Lords of the Council to sign the new bond, they undertaking in it to become "the King's true Subjects," and being bound over in as "good Surety as could be devised by the Laws," and receiving in return their pardons. On Monday, however, the Deputy informed the Commissioner that it would be advisable in his opinion that the oaths should be taken at Maynooth Castle, instead of in Dublin. It was a more convenient spot, he said, for the distant members of the Council to assemble in. In short, better in every way.

Sir Richard remonstrated indignantly, but Geroit Mor was not to be withstood. It was indispensable, he said, that he should go to Maynooth himself at once, and it was equally indispensable that Sir Richard should go there with him as his guest. It went to his honour that the King's Chamberlain and High Commissioner should lodge under any roof but his own. In vain Sir Richard protested against this somewhat belated hospitality. In vain he pointed out that Dublin, not Maynooth, was supposed to be the seat of the Irish Government. He might have spared his breath. The Earl of Kildare's mind was made up, and the rest of the world had nothing to do but to obey.

The irregularity of the proceeding was enough to turn any courtier's hair grey, but there was no help for it. The Lords of the Council were all getting upon their horses, and starting across the fields for Maynooth. The King's Commissioner was forced to mount and depart also, carrying his pardons, and his other official gear, along with him.

The road between Thomas Court and the castle of Maynooth must have been a tolerably well frequented one in those days. The distance was only about a dozen miles, and there was a fair road in summer-time, if you chose to keep to it, and at all times a pleasant green plain to ride over. Thither rode the Earl and the Commissioner side by side, followed by their respective trains, and in a short time the fires in the castle were blazing, the boards spread, and Sir Richard was being regaled, as he himself admitted, with much " righte good Cheer." This was upon the 14th of July, and upon the 15th, we have the satisfaction of knowing that Sir Richard " had agen gret Cheer of the Erle." The members of the Council had by this time nearly all assembled at Maynooth, and they and Kildare were observed to hold " gret Communications among themselves." Further than this, nothing however was done. So the 15th and the 16th passed. Upon the 17th, the Commissioner's patience fairly boiled over. Did they intend to sign the bond, or did they not? he wanted to know, speaking, he tells us, " with righte fell and angry Words." The same afternoon he again told them " righte plainly and

sharply of their unfitting Demeaning," the result of which remonstrance was that the whole
party got upon their horses, and rode back
to Dublin, having so far achieved absolutely
nothing.

Next day, the 18th of July, matters came
to a climax. The members of the Council had
now thoroughly made up their minds. They
were *not* going to sign the bond, and so they
told Sir Richard plainly. They were sorry to
displease him, but it was out of the question.
Anything else they were willing to do, but
not this, and that for an excellent, though un-
avowable reason. If they did, all their estates
would be forfeited to the King upon the next
little occasion of the kind. In vain the Commissioner threatened them with his master's
displeasure. They replied that they were ready
to take oath to become the King's true lieges,
and to be bound over "in good Suretys," such
as he might approve of, but sign such a bond
they would not. Rather than that they would
prefer to become "Irysh, every one of them."

This formidable threat seems to have settled
the matter. Sir Richard was forced to give in.
Possibly he may have received instructions that
he might do so if he found the particular point
impossible to carry. In any case he now drew

up such a form of oath as he considered to be the most binding under the circumstances, and sent it to the Lords for their approval. This was upon the 19th. Next day it was agreed to, and the whole party met in council in the "King's Chambir" at Thomas Court. Here the Earl of Kildare went through the form of homage to Sir Richard Edgecombe, as representing the King, the rest of the Lords of the Council following suit. A gold chain, "the Collar of the King's Livery," was laid upon the Earl's neck, and mass was said, Sir Richard being particularly careful to have the elements consecrated by his own chaplain. After this the whole party adjourned to the church of the monastery, where a Te Deum was said, the bells of the church were rung, "and the Choir with the Organs sung it up solemnly." The ceremony wound up by a dinner given at the Friary.

Thankful to have finished the matter on any terms, the Commissioner next day rode to Drogheda, from whence he returned upon the 28th, and on the 29th Kildare handed in his certificate of allegiance, duly signed and witnessed, and received in return the King's pardon under the Great Seal. This was the last scene. Reconciliation and loyalty were now supposed to have settled down for good upon Ireland.

All who had taken part in the late Simnel rising were to be forgiven, with the exception of Keating, the prior of Kilmainham, whose offence appears to have been regarded as peculiarly heinous, though how he can have steeped himself much deeper in treason than the rest of his neighbours it is not very easy to see.

Eager to avoid further delays, Sir Richard rode off the same day to Dalkey, where his ships were lying at anchor. The winds, however, he tells us in his diary, were again " contraryous," and he had to remain there for nearly another week. At last he sailed, and after eight days' tossing, and many " perillous jeopardies," landed once more in Cornwall. Here—by way perhaps of thanksgiving for having ever returned at all—he in his turn went upon a pilgrimage to the " Chappell of Saint Saviour," at that time the most highly reputed of all Cornish shrines. And so the long tragi-comedy of Rebellion and Pardon came to an end.

And here too for us the story of Geroit Mor must end, although his further adventures will be found to be at least equally well worth following. They must be looked for, however, in the right place, seeing that the little space which remains to us is required for the adventures of another Irish hero, in whose history, even more than in that of the great Geraldine, we find traces of that all-saving admixture of the humorous, which is elsewhere in Irish history so lamentably and so inexplicably wanting.

Wherein the point of this particular jest lies it may be as well to explain, seeing that no two people have ever yet agreed as to what is or is not humorous. To my mind, then, it lies mainly in the fact of the relative strength and import-ance of the two antagonists who appear before us. These two were—on the one hand that picturesque, if rather flowery and ineffectual personage, Richard II., King of England, Wales, and France; Lord of Acquitaine, Ireland, and a few other principalities, backed by an army of nearly thirty thousand men—a pro-digiously fine force, it will be understood, for those days. On the other hand there was his own rebellious subject, Arthur Kavanagh of Wexford; known to his familiars as Art, to his tribesmen as the MacMurrough, and to his flatterers as the King of Leinster; the undisputed ruler of some fourteen or fifteen hundred gallo-glasses, mostly without shoes or stockings, all without proper arms or training. Nor is the point of the jest blunted by the fact that it was the latter, and not the former, who eventually remained master of the field.

Froissart, who rarely falls below his opportunities for picturesque reporting, and who has left us a number of very piquant details with regard to King Richard and his Court, stints us of our meed of gossip when that monarch goes to Ireland. This was unavoidable, seeing that the great chronicler never himself set foot in that island, and was obliged to fall back upon second-hand, and consequently inferior, information. The most trustworthy of his informants appears to have been one Castide, a gentleman originally in the train of the Earl of Ormond, who having been taken prisoner by the Irish, and retained by them for some time, was able for the rest of his life to fill the responsible post of interpreter to the Irish Court. In spite of having married a Wexford woman during his captivity, his bias is clearly of the Pale all compact, and must be taken therefore with due caution. Between the lines we may however, I think, discern a more or less vivid picture of the times, and in any case must be thankful in these matters for what we can get. Here, then, as I read it,—possibly not quite accurately !— runs the tale.

R

THE SONG
OF ART KAVANAGH

Oh, 'tis well to be a king's heir, and ride across
    the land
With twenty score of archers, and knights on
    either hand.
Sing the battle song of Art!

But the fighting men of Wexford know how
    to use the sword,
And the loyal knights of Mortimer are seek-
    ing for their lord!
Sing the battle song of Art!

Oh, 'tis well to be a king, and to sail across
    the sea
With twenty thousand archers, and great lords
    at your knee.
Sing the battle song of Art!

But the Wexford woods are deep, and the
    Wexford trees are tall,
And when next their leaves are falling they
    may cover one and all!
Sing the battle song of Art!

HOW ART KAVANAGH OF WEXFORD
FOUGHT RICHARD THE KING

I

THE Pale was all on fire again ! There had
been raids at Rathcoole, at Newcastle, and at
the Naas ; raids at Trim, at Dunshauglin, and
over the greater part of Fingal. The O'Byrnes,
the O'Keefes, the O'Nolans, were all out, and
swarming over the country like hornets. Calvagh
O'Toole, who not long before had assailed the
English in Leinster, and had caused " six score
of their heads," says his native chronicler, " to
be carried in triumph before him," was again
upon the war-path and might be expected to
repeat that performance. Worse still, Art
Kavanagh was known to have recently left his
head-quarters at Wexford, and to be out somewhere with all his young men at his heels, and
though nobody upon the English side knew

exactly where he was, that only made matters more unpleasant, since wherever you would wish him not to be, there you might be certain he would presently be found.

Barely three years had come and gone since King Richard himself had left Ireland, having remained there for ten months, and held high state in Dublin, feasting himself and others, as a king should do. To him had come all the greater chiefs, who, having sworn fealty, had accepted knighthood at his hands ; not, it must be said, without some demur on their part, they declaring loudly that knighthood in their country was invariably bestowed at the age of ten, or even younger—so soon, in fact, as a lad had shown any signs of spirit—and that it was a toy therefore, unfit for grown men and bearded warriors. Seeing, however, that Ard-Righ made such a point of the matter, they in the end submitted with a fairly good grace, even Art Kavanagh keeping his vigils—the grim penitent! —in Christ Church Cathedral. Next day, " clad in a silk garment edged with fur," he had been feasted at the King's own table, with the O'Neil from the North on his right hand, and the O'Connor Faley from mid-Leinster on his left, while Mr. Interpreter Castide, through whose eyes Froissart saw the scene, and has described it to us, bustled from one chief to another, anxious that his pupils should do credit to his instructions on this great occasion. The English Privy Council meanwhile were writing to congratulate their lord the King upon the success with which he had won over "le O'Nel," and that still more desperate person "le grand Macmourg." The monarch himself, clad in a "cote of gold and stone," and looking as comely as a prince in a fairy tale, smiling no doubt, and reflecting upon how easy it was to manage this country, so long as you had the sense to come over to it yourself, and not trust everything, as his grandfather had done, to fellows like De Bracy, or De Courcy, or De Burgh, whose interest it was to make the worst of every trifling disorder, the better to magnify their own office, and the larger amount to extort out of your already cruelly deplenished treasury.

All this was quite as it ought to be, but then it was already three whole years ago, and three years leave room for a good many disastrous changes, especially in Ireland ! It was Richard himself who began the mischief by being foolish enough to put Art in prison for some trifling offence whilst still his guest ; and although the imprisonment had been but nominal, it had been quite enough to infuriate that fiery warrior, and thoroughly to undo any impression which might have been produced upon him by previous civilities.

Like many great personages, Richard, however, never believed in harm accruing from any action which he personally was good enough to undertake. Accordingly he sailed away to England with great complacency, to see after the Lollards, who were known to be badly in need just then of burning, leaving his cousin, Roger of March, to look after this part of his kingdom in his absence; to follow in his own footsteps, and generally to manage Ireland in the manner approved by those who had the charge of her.

A very important young man was Roger, Earl of March, seeing that by right of his mother he nominally owned the greater part of Ulster, with a large slice of Connaught to boot. Indeed, if he could have come by his rights, a good fifth of Ireland would at that moment have been his private property, not to mention that, upon the death of his cousin Richard, he was bound to succeed to the crown of England, with all the pleasant things thereto appertaining.

Out of Dublin he rode upon a certain morning early in July, full of hope and confidence, and many knights with him, and a long train of

soldiery stretching after them like the tail of a
comet. Seldom had a gallanter party ridden
out of those gates, or one in better spirits ; for,
so far as they knew, they had only the O'Tooles
and the O'Byrnes in front of them, who might
be expected to run like their own mountain
sheep at the mere wind and whiff of all those
gleaming swords. Yet the looks of the few
people they passed were more scowling than
admiring, and there was less fear than hate in
their eyes. And one old hag, as they rode past
her cabin, getting upon a log of wood, cried
shrilly, "*Vo ! vo ! Manam an diaoul*, but I can
see the skean that is lifted to slit that white
skin of yours ! *Manam an diaoul*, I know
one that will outrun that horse of yours, and
will pluck you from it and crush you, as I might
crush a ripe droneen upon the bogs. *Vo ! vo !
Manam an diaoul ! Manam an diaoul !*"

So she screeched, looking straight at the
young Viceroy. Happily it was all in Irish,
so that he and the knights merely smiled, and
observed to one another in Norman-French that
our lord the King had queer subjects upon this
side of the Channel, and that such an ill-
looking crone as yonder were better tossed into
a bog-hole to see would she sink, which, judging
by her looks, seemed scarce probable. Soon

they forgot her, however, having more important matters on hand, and so reached the castle under whose roof the first night of their expedition was to be spent.   Here the horses were unsaddled ; the men-at-arms bustled about, and Roger and his knights gathered into the central hall, where a fire was lit, for, though the month was July, it was damp enough. And they ate, and they drank, and made such merriment as they could, while the ghost of the former inhabitants of the place scurried away into dark corners, not liking such goings on.

So all went well, and promised well for the morrow.   About seven o'clock the same evening, however, there came a sudden rattling at the outer gates, and six kerns belonging to the nearest loyalist, a good man but a timid one, rushed in, their cheeks hanging with terror, to say that Art MacMurrough of Wexford had appeared with all his men, and had been seen from the top of the nearest hill ; that he was burning all the villages before him, and that at the rate he was travelling, he would probably by this time have got as far as Kells.

Now this was perfectly unexpected news, and unexpected things are rarely pleasant ones, especially in Ireland.   Nevertheless, Roger Mor-

timer rose to the occasion, and showed no
unbecoming discomfiture. He was not a particularly brilliant young man, so far as has been
recorded ; still he was a Plantagenet, and it was
not likely that any Plantagenet would turn
tail before even the wildest of wild Irishmen.
Accordingly he summoned his armourer, and
ordered his war harness to be gone over, and all
its joints duly tried. And he called a council of
war, and arranged that all should be in readiness
to start early the next morning. And by five
o'clock, no later—for even self-indulgent young
gentlemen, and heirs to a kingdom, had to be
bustling in those days—he was in the saddle,
and spurring fast along the way, with all his
merry men following close behind him.

II

WHETHER Roger of March's horse stumbled
that morning as he was starting, or whether a
single crow flew across his path, or whether his
nose bled, or his sword slipped out of its scabbard,
or what other portents befell him cannot now
be known, though no doubt the chroniclers of
the day must have recorded them in the fullest
detail, since it is impossible that any one so

important could have got into such serious
trouble without something of the sort happening to warn him. When he had ridden about
a dozen miles he caused his men to halt,
for they were coming to an awkward bit of
country. A considerable bog lay in front of
them, which would not at all suit the horses,
and was about as unpleasant a place as it was
possible for a knight in armour to get over-
thrown in, since there he was likely to lie like
a turtle, getting deeper and deeper the more
he struggled to escape, till perhaps some Irishman with a skean came along that way, to make
matters worse.

Westward, where the ground was firmer, lay
a wood ; not a large one, but still thick enough
not to be able to be seen through. Now it was
a point of some importance to ascertain whether
Art Kavanagh and the O'Tooles had as yet
joined forces, since, if they had not done so, it
would be much easier to fight them separately ;
nay, they might even save trouble by first
fighting one another, leaving only the victor
to be dealt with. Unfortunately there was a
great dearth of spies just then upon the King's
side, but some turf-cutters they had captured had
reported that a large body of Irish was lying in
wait for the Viceroy in a wood upon the other

side of a bog. Was this the place meant, and if so, what sized force could be lying concealed there? The Viceroy held a hasty council, consisting chiefly of young men—for he had few others with him — and the unanimous decision they arrived at was that no force of any size could possibly be concealed in such a place; the wood being, as was plain to be seen, so thin, and the region around it so clear, and so open.

Now this only shows the disadvantage of fighting in a country with which you are imperfectly acquainted, as well as against foes of whose mode of warfare all you know is that it is utterly savage, and quite unworthy the consideration of a knight and a Plantagenet! Scarcely had Roger and his soldiers advanced towards the wood before there arose a howl from it as if all the wolves in Ireland were breaking loose. And out of the wood rushed a crowd of foot-soldiers, and down they came towards where the heir of England was advancing, with all his knights behind him, and that unpleasant, squelching bog immediately in front of them. After these came a crowd of wild horsemen, who had been hidden behind a ridge of scraws, each man riding his chief war-horse, worth at the very least two hundred cows apiece.

Saddleless they rode, with brass bits, and sliding reins, and in front of them rode a horseman upon a big black horse, which was known throughout the length and breadth of Ireland. Coal-black was its colour, and it stood over eighteen hands high, and its name in Irish was ten syllables long, and meant " The Tree Leaper," and its value was reported to be six hundred cows, or rather that would have been its value, only that Art Kavanagh got it for nothing, having carried it off from its owner upon one of his Munster raids.

Upon the Tree Leaper rode Art himself, carrying a big, iron-tipped spear in his hands. " A man of great stature, very fell and ferocious to the eye," says Castide, who knew him well. " He rode," says another eye-witness, describing him at Arklow, " so that never in all my life, I declare to you, did I see hare, sheep, deer, or any other animal run with such speed." In this fashion he rode now ; with his horsemen following behind him, and the kerns and galloglasses swarming barefooted towards the bog. As for the English, caught in this very uncomfortable trap, they tried to steady themselves, and wished no doubt with all their hearts for a good bit of firm ground—" long heath, brown furze, any-thing," so that they could only find their feet

solidly beneath them. Young Roger put himself gallantly in front of his men, and presently,
with a clash that was heard three miles away,
the two forces closed, and such was the confusion that for a time no one knew how the
battle went, or who had the best of it, for everything was a tangle, and wild bewilderment ; with
horses rearing, and swords clashing, and spears
flashing, and all the tug and actual physical
contact of war, as it existed before big cannons
and Enfield rifles came to spoil it. Presently,
however, there was a lull, for the Irish fashion
of fighting was to make one of these tremendous
rushes, and then to draw back and prepare for
another. Back went Art to the wood, and his
men after him, leaving a clear space, heaped up
with the dead and the dying. And then there
arose a long, loud cry upon the royal side, for
—alas for the hopes of England ! — amongst
those who were lying face uppermost upon the
soil was no less a personage than the Heir
Apparent himself !

A dozen knights flew to pick him up, but
too late, for his blood was flowing fast, and
Art's big, iron-tipped spear was sticking out of
his side a little way above the heart. And
whether he uttered any last words must be left
to be guessed, but most likely he uttered none,

but met his death as every man must, whether
out of doors with his armour on, or in bed with
the blankets smoothed round his chin.   Indeed
there was scant leisure for any leave-taking, for
before any one could breathe, Art MacMurrough was out of the wood again, and was charg-
ing more furiously than before.   And this time,
whether from finding themselves overmatched,
or from not liking the nature of the ground, or
from discouragement at the death of their leader,
the English waited no longer, but fled at full
speed.   And many fell into the bog, and were
slain, and many more were overtaken, and killed
in the open, and only the best mounted, cutting
their way past Art, rode back the way they
had come, and in due time reached Dublin.
Here, the gates being flung open for them,
in they went, the first that entered carrying
with him the dead body of young Roger of
March, hanging limply, head downwards, over
his saddle-bow.

III

LET the reader imagine for himself the return
of Art Kavanagh to Wexford after these events!
Let him picture the march through the inter-

vening glades; the exultant tribesmen laden with
booty, driving before them herds swept from the
" obedient shires" to swell their own droves;
the triumphant screeching of the bagpipes, the
wild whooping, the hurroushing. Then, as they
drew nearer home, let him picture the rushing
out of the women, their yellow cloaks floating
behind them, their hair flying in the wind.
Truly a great day for Wexford! almost great
enough to wash out the stain of the invasion,
since had Ireland never been invaded, the heir
to the crown of England could clearly never have
fallen beneath the spear of the MacMurrough.

But that doughty warrior himself was no fool,
and he knew very well that England was not
utterly out of reach, and that a day of reckoning
would come, and that, when it came, it would
probably be an awkward one to meet. He cast
about therefore for some combination which
could be brought to bear upon the common
enemy; not an easy thing to find in a country
where no two chiefs ever combined together for
a week without becoming deadly foes before
the Sunday morning.

In the end he made up his mind to send to
Turlough O'Brien, son of Murrough-na-Raithnighe O'Brien, Prince of Thomond, who was sib
to himself upon the mother's side, and to urge

him to get ready all his young men, so as to be able at any moment to sally across the Shannon upon the Butlers, thereby creating a diversion. For this errand it was necessary to choose a messenger with some care, for between Wexford and Thomond lay the whole width of Ireland, a tract beset with worse snares for travellers than probably any similar extent of mid-Africa to-day. The messenger he finally decided to send was his own foster brother's son, Felim, the son of Liag. Having mounted him, therefore, upon the best horse, next to the Tree Leaper, in his possession—a raw-boned bay, with the temper of a fiend, but the speed of an Arab, and the endurance of an ox—and having taught him the message he was to deliver, he sent him on his way with this parting injunction :

"Repeat what I have said to Turlough, son of Murrough-na-Raithnighe, and sixty cows and thrice sixty calves are thine on thy return. Miss it by one word, and thy head joins those" —a row of grisly mementoes of the late raid— "and all thine with thee. I, Art, the son of Art, have spoken."

Hearing this, Felim MacLiag probably laughed, and rode off in the best of spirits, for as for those parting threats, they were only the common amenities of the time, and meant no more than that he was to do his best, and not loiter too long by the road.

On he went over the undulating country, till he came to the river Barrow, which he crossed by the ford called Graiguenamanagh. And now he had to go warily, for this was the boundary of the Ormond country, and since Art's capture of New Ross, or Ros-mic-Triuin, as it was then called, a messenger of his would have fared extremely badly in Butler hands.

Soon he was out upon the level country, with the broad limestone plain of Ireland lying around him; one green esker after another stretching away like Atlantic waves that had grown stiff and grassy. As he rode along, the cattle raced away like deer before him. There were no sheep, for unless protected by sheep-folds, their only use would have been to feed the wolves. Crows, stalking over the grass, rose with hoarse caws as he galloped towards them. Magpies there were none, nor yet a single frog in any of the pools, for neither of these were introduced until many a century later.

By noon he came to the beginning of the forest country. And here, in native parlance, he had to wear his eyes upon sticks, for the wood kerns in those parts were remarkably

s

awkward people to meet with, whether nominally under the rule of the great house of
Ormond, or merely reiving and raiding on their
own account. And well was it for him that he
was on the alert, for, before he had ridden a
mile under the boughs, six big fellows sprang
at him, shouting "Butler a boo!" and one
made a clutch at his rein, and the rest flung a
shower of knives at him, and although he rode
for his life, and in the end got away from them,
one of the knives stuck fast, and, when he
looked down, there it was sticking like a big
thorn in his bridle arm.

After this he had to cross another river, and
make a long circuit to avoid more Butlers.
And about six in the evening, his arm being
sore, and the stock of food he had started with
exhausted, he ventured to stop at a village;
knowing that he was probably by this time in
the country of the O'Carrols, who, as it
happened, were just then friendly with Art.

The village lay in the centre of the forest,
the houses being built wholly of wood, con-
structed beehive fashion, round a stake in the
centre, and wattled; the chinks being filled up
with mud. Here the dogs barked at him, and
the children hooted, but the women drove them
away, and gave him food—oaten bread and a

bit of meat—after which, fearing to delay, he
rode on again till nine o'clock, when it grew
too dark to enable him to make his way.
Accordingly he dismounted, and lay down to
sleep, with the bay cropping near him, and glad
enough, no doubt, by this time to be allowed to
stand still.

Felim awoke, however, before the first streaks
of dawn were beginning to peer over the tree-
tops. And very likely he wished for some
breakfast, but having none, was forced to go on
without any, and, having no saddle to put on
the bay, he simply leapt upon its back, and
away again as fast as he could go to the west.
And in the course of time he perceived the
Shannon spreading below him, and so got to
O'Brien's bridge, at that time the only one in
those parts, and a bad bridge for any man who was
not a friend of the O'Briens to attempt to cross.
And not long after crossing it he found himself
amongst the stony wastes, and bright blue lakes,
of Thomond, with the Atlantic sleeping in the
distance ; by which time both the bay and himself must have felt as if a considerable time had
passed over their heads since they started so
blithely from Wexford.

IV

AND now another year has come and gone, and great events are happening upon the other side of the island. King Richard himself has come again ; sailing over from England with such a convoy of ships, such a muster of knights, and such a gathering of archers and men-at-arms as never were seen before in Ireland, and has anchored under the walls of Waterford. And now everybody believed that Art Kavanagh's hour had surely come !

Nothing could appear to be more convenient, either, than such a landing-place. The rebel's country was close at hand. A few hours' riding, and that ragged forest edge, behind which he was known to be ensconced, lay full in sight.

Was Art panic-stricken ? Was he struck helpless at the sight of this great armament gathered together to crush him ? It looked at first as though he were. Not a sign of life did he give, not a kern of his showed, not a single horseman was to be seen. Even the town of Carlow, which he had held for the last two years, was left undefended, ready for the new-comers to take possession of. The entire region seemed to have grown suddenly depopulated. Where

a few weeks before great herds of cattle were
grazing, with bare-legged urchins at their heels,
not a sign now of boys or of beasts was to be
seen. The King had apparently nothing to do
but to make a progress over the country, and
then retire to Dublin, having attained all that
he came to Ireland to accomplish.

Unfortunately for himself that highly ornamental monarch was utterly deficient in all the
qualities that go to make a leader, " loving best,"
as an historian of the day tells us, " those coun-
cillors which did advise him worst." Disorder
was at that moment rampant behind him in
England. The law was utterly in abeyance ;
highwaymen abounded ; farmers were pillaged ;
bishops and great lords were forced to take refuge
in the towns from the disorders of the country.
People, we are told by the same historian, were
everywhere saying openly, "We have a good-
for-nothing King, and the time is come that we
seek for a remedy." The Londoners, who from
various causes were just then in the ascendant,
especially complained. "They spoke one to
another," says Froissart, "of what had happened in the second Edward's time, for the
children of those days, become men, had often
been told about them by their fathers, and
others had read them in the chronicles of the

times, and they said openly: 'They provided a remedy, and now it is our turn.'"

How far Art knew of all this, and knew, therefore, that time would prove his best friend, or how far he merely followed his own time-immemorial fashion of warfare, must be left to be guessed. Certain it is that during the next six weeks he led Richard of Bordeaux a pretty dance amongst those Wexford and Carlow woods! The King "sat down" before them, but trees not being forts, the sitting down process produced no very perceptible results. His huge army of 20,000 archers and 4000 men-at-arms presently began to starve. Then an order was given for them to advance, and the big, unwieldy mass did try to advance, but got promptly entangled in the coppices, and all but lost in the blinding jungle of trees, where never yet an axe had swung, or a saw been plied. The King swore that he would cut down the whole forest, but it may easily be guessed how far he got in *that* operation. He had not much local advice to fall back upon either, for Felim MacLiag's mission had prospered to the uttermost, and the O'Briens had long ere this come swarming across their bridge, and were giving the Butlers, and other loyalists in mid-Leinster, quite as much as they could do to hold their own, without lending any help to their master.

Seeing how matters were going, Art presently began to sally out, and take the initiative. He had barely 3000 men with him, but then he was at home, and, in such warfare as this, that is an advantage which outweighs nearly all others. As the King's army moved on he waylaid the stragglers, much as the Russians waylaid the French after Moscow, and cut them off by the score. One night he gained a more considerable advantage. Four hundred archers had been posted about a mile from the main force. Upon these Art fell silently at early dawn, and although the men with him at the time were actually fewer in number than their antagonists, such was the confusion, and such the intricacy of the forest, that only a few archers escaped, and rushed, bleeding and panic-stricken, to the English camp to tell the news.

Out came King Richard himself, we are told, on hearing the commotion, clad in a gorgeous loose surcoat, embroidered with golden ears of wheat. And when he heard what had happened, and when, going later in the day to the place, he found not a trace of Art, but only his own men lying dead one upon the other, then he broke into very unkingly cursing, and vowed that if ever he caught that pernicious traitor, there should not be a town in Ireland— no, nor in England either—but should have a piece of him to decorate its gates with.

Cursing, however, mended nothing, and as for his unhappy soldiers, they were beginning by this time to die off like flies from want of food, as well as from cold, and damp, and dysentery; while those that remained were so weakened that they fell all the easier prey to Art's young men, who lay in wait for them in every direction in the forest, and cut off all that they could find. The sentries especially they cut off, so that of a morning, when they had to be relieved, it was generally found that there was no occasion to do anything of the sort, for they lay perfectly still and silent, and would clearly never feel cold, or hunger, or curse the Irish service again in this world.

Picture to yourself the huge heterogeneous host, such as always in those days accompanied a king on his travels ! Not alone soldiers, by any means; but also courtiers, and secretaries; churchmen, and politicians; suitors, dicers, hucksters, singers, barbers; human odds and ends of every kind, all gathered together in such a place, and under such circumstances ! Six mortal weeks they remained in those weary

Wexford woods. Rained upon ; blown upon ;
never having a chance of striking an open blow
at their foes ; with hardly any food ; without,
for the most part, the slightest arrangement as
to sleeping quarters. Richard himself had his
tent, but the rest might lie as they could.
Sometimes at dead of night the cry would be
raised that Art was upon them. Then might
have been heard a wild scurrying, and a clatter
of armour, as, out of holes of the earth, or the
hollows of trees, grim, warlike figures began
to arise ; and swords were buckled on with
stiff fingers ; and many curses, in many
tongues, rose to the low, dark Irish sky
overhead !

Even when no night surprises occurred,
matters were hardly better. Art Kavanagh
might relax, but the weather never relaxed.
Never in the memory of man had there been
such a season ! The whole camp was one vast
swamp. The horses had only green oats to eat ;
their less fortunate riders, not so much. The
provision ships, which had formed part of the
fleet, had sailed away, nobody seems to have
known whither, and knightly men fought one
another for scraps which two months earlier
their own dogs would have rejected.

From bad, matters grew to worse. Provisions of all sorts were nearly at an end, and no fresh ones were procurable. The country around seemed to be a desert, and famine in its worst form was staring every one in the face. At last, in despair, an order was given to start for the coast. The point to be attained was Arklow, and the army moved thither, at first with some appearance of order. Famine, however, is a sad corrupter of discipline. The soldiers broke line ; straggled away whenever a chance of food, a hint of a hen-roost, the hope even of a few handfuls of bilberries, presented itself. By the time the village was reached the King's great army had become a mere mob— hungry, miserable, disorganized. Pell-mell they rushed into it, and proceeded to ransack it to the uttermost. But its resources were easily exhausted. The cattle had all long since been driven away. The few inhabitants left in it stared helplessly, or fell grovelling upon their knees in terror before their depredators.

Suddenly a cry arose that the provision ships had been seen sailing round Greenore Point ! Like an avalanche the hungry host rushed out of the village, and proceeded to pour itself over the sand-hills to the sea. There, sure enough, were the ships, but the wind was contrary, and it seemed doubtful whether they would be able to make the shore, even if they realized the imminence of the need for them. The excitement grew desperate. Fires were lighted on the heights. Signals of distress were shown. Men ran wildly to and fro, scarce knowing what they did. Others—past this stage—lay staring with haggard eyes upon the ships. The sands were strewn with men, dying with the provisions they needed in sight. When at length the three vessels did approach to shore they were met in the water by the famine-stricken soldiers, who waded up to their necks to get at the food. " Very great contention was there," says an eye-witness of the scene, " to get a share of it. Every man spent his half-penny or his penny on himself ; some in eating, some in drinking ; thus the whole was devoured very speedily." [1]

At last Richard's pride broke down. While the ships still hung doubtfully in the bay he sent to demand a parley with Art. If that contumacious rebel could be induced to come to terms, the strain of the situation would be relaxed. Cattle would be obtainable ; his

[1] For further details of this very odd scene, read " A French Metrical History of the Deposition of King Richard the Second," of which a translation will be found in Vol. XX. of *The Archæologia.*

starving army could be fed ; he himself would be able to fall back upon Dublin.

Probably Art knew all this at least as well as did King Richard, for his terms rose steadily. He consented to hold a parley with the Earl of Gloucester, but his tone was that of an equal, not of a repentant rebel. He would make peace, he said, with the King, but it must be a peace without reservations. All that he had already seized upon he was to be allowed to keep. The disputed lands in Kildare, which he claimed in right of his wife, were to be handed over to him. The O'Briens, his allies, were not to be molested. His own title of King of Leinster was to be formally recognized. Richard swore by St. Edward that he would remain in Ireland all the days of his life rather than agree to such terms as those, and ordered Gloucester to return to Art, and command him to appear at once before him in Dublin, whither he was then going.

Gloucester, however, avoided doing anything of the sort, doubting probably the wisdom of the proceeding, but instead he sent an humbler messenger, whose throat, if Art cut it, would be of much less consequence. This second messenger found that redoubtable rebel feasting in the open air in the middle of the forest, like

an Irish Robin Hood, with all his clan about
him. To him he delivered the King's message,
which Art received sitting crossed-legged ; with
his private chaplain upon one side of him, and
his harper upon the other, as may be seen in
the illuminations of the day.

Then, when the interpreter had finished
expounding the King's message, Art replied
to this effect—

" Bid your lord," said he scornfully, " command his own kerns, and not meddle with me
or mine. If he wanted me in Dublin why did
he not take me there ? Six weeks had he to do
it in, yet here I, Art, still sit. Tell him, too,
that the air of Wexford agreeth not, methinks,
with his young men, for they were very fresh
and lusty of aspect when they came to it,
whereas they lie now for the most part green,
sad, and very mouldy under our feet ! "

" True ! true ! Hurrah for Art Mac-
Murrough ! " shouted the clansmen delight-
edly.

" Tell him too," pursued Art, warming under
the breath of that popular applause, " that I
have eaten before of his meat, and have drank
before of his cup, and that, though the flavour
of both was good at the time, yet I liked not

the after-taste of the same. Tell him that
King of Leinster, I, Art MacMurrough, was
born, and that King of Leinster, I, Art, intend
to die, and that it were well for him if he
could say the same of that kingdom of his
beyond the wave. Tell him, moreover "—
here Art's aspect became so terrific that the
messenger nearly died of fright—" that I spare
you, because I require you to yelp your errand
into his ear, but that the next slave he sends
to me will travel back to Dublin without eyes
to find the way, without hands to grope along
the paths, and without a tongue with which
to insult the MacMurrough. I, Art, the son
of Art, have spoken !"

Then that messenger returned, with his
teeth chattering, and his knees knocking woe-
fully against one another, and having, to his
own surprise, got alive to Dublin, he told
what had been said to him to the King.

"By the eyes of God," exclaimed Richard,
"this fellow's insolence exceedeth belief. As I
am a king I will yet cut down that wood of
his, and will hang him up for a mawkin upon
the last bough of the same !" and he looked
for the moment like a Plantagenet as he
said it.

It was not to be, however, for worse things than even Art's insults were at that moment hanging over his head. And only a week later, upon the Sunday morning, as he was coming out of mass, there met him Bagot, and two other messengers from the Duke of York, to tell him that his cousin, Henry of Hereford, had landed at Ravensburg, and that all England was gathering to him like one man.

Richard's usually ruddy face grew suddenly grey, we are told, at this news. Confident, however, in his own charm, and in that divinity which hedges kings, he even then delayed his departure for another fortnight. God, he told those who urged him to set off at once, would assuredly fight for His Richard, and England, he was privately convinced, would never have the heart to turn her back upon one whom she had certainly formerly loved. Here, however, as we are aware, he deceived himself. " Alack for woe, that any harm should stain so fair a show ! " Richard's England had had enough of him, and preferred for the moment some one who would at least show her a little variety in the way of bad government. So, having delayed just long enough to make his cause absolutely hopeless, he at last returned, to meet the fate that was in store for him. But Art Kavanagh remained behind at home in Wexford, and ruled over his own lands, as he had predicted, until his death.

THE END

Richard Clay & Sons, Limited, London & Bungay.

The List of Titles
in the Garland Series

MARIA EDGEWORTH

1. Castle Rackrent *(1800)*
2. An Essay on Irish Bulls *(1802)*
3. Ennui *(1809)*
4. The Absentee *(1812)*
5. Ormond *(1817)*

SYDNEY OWENSON, LADY MORGAN

6. The Wild Irish Girl *(1806)*
7. O'Donnel. A National Tale *(1814)*
8. Florence Macarthy: an Irish Tale *(1818)*
9. The O'Briens and the O'Flahertys *(1817)*
10. Dramatic Sketches from Real Life *(1833)*

CHARLES ROBERT MATURIN

11. The Wild Irish Boy *(1808)*
12. The Milesian Chief *(1812)*
13. Women; or, Pour et Contre: A Tale *(1818)*

ANTHONY TROLLOPE

JOSEPH SHERIDAN LE FANU

WILLIAM ALLINGHAM

CHARLOTTE RIDDELL (MRS. J.H. RIDDELL)

EMILY LAWLESS

WILLIAM O'BRIEN

ANONYMOUS